U0084416

苦練出來的語言最美

　　全世界都知道，傳統英語教學最大的缺點，就是學了不會說。多少人從小學到大學，努力學英文，學了幾十年，還是不會開口說。少數會說幾句英語的人，說起來沒有信心，結結巴巴，因為不知道自己說的對還是錯，大多不敢張開嘴巴，有信心地大聲說。

　　小孩子記憶力強，背東西背得快，但是忘得也快。「一口氣兒童英語演講」有固定格式，孩子可以一篇接一篇地背下去。只要將「一口氣兒童英語演講①②」背完，就能夠連續講英文 30 分鐘以上，腦筋裡面就儲存了 540 個句子，可以做無限多的排列組合，每個句子背熟後，就會變成一個句型，可以舉一反三。

　　背單字不如背句子，背了單字不見得會用，背了句子馬上就可以用。背一個句子會忘，背三個句子也會忘，連續背九個句子，串連在一起，就不容易忘記。「一口氣英語」系列，每一回九句，每一本十二回，共 108 句，孩子們背完之後，就可以和外國人做簡單的交談。

　　學語言最大的困難是，學了會忘記，學了等於白學。有了「一口氣英語」後，只要將每一本「一口氣英語」，背到一分鐘之內，就終生不會忘記。背了十本，就有 1080 句，從小開始背，日積月累下來，不得了。

會用英語演講，能增加領袖氣質

「一口氣兒童英語演講」內容全部取材自美國口語的精華，可利用演講中的內容，和外國人深談，也可寫出動人的文章。一般美國人寫文章會錯，但你用「一口氣兒童英語演講」中的句子，組合成文章，就非常精彩了。

小孩子從小養成背英語演講的習慣，有了目標，腦筋不會亂想，一篇接一篇地背下去，很有成就感。演講中的內容，無形中也陶冶了身心。從小就會上台用英語演講，長大就不得了，可以成為國際級的領袖人物。

很多父母為了讓小孩學英文，把小孩送到國外去，想不到，一些小留學生回國後，說起英文來，像是含在嘴巴裡一樣，說得模模糊糊，畏畏縮縮。可能是因為他們從小在國外，和外國小孩在一起，總怕講錯話，養成嘴巴張不開的習慣。更糟糕的是，受到外國文化的影響，不中不西，一不小心，就變成邊緣人。

但是，如果背了「一口氣英語演講」，就不一樣了。「一口氣英語演講」中的每個句子，都是經過精挑細選，你說的每一句話，都是苦練過的，說起來自然有信心，自然會張開嘴巴，清清楚楚，一句一句地大聲說出來。能夠站在台上慷慨激昂地發表演說，就具有成為領袖或大人物的特質。

劉 毅

CONTENTS

1. My Favorite Class

1

My favorite class is gym.
I can't wait for PE.
It's really fun, fun, fun.

I love to get out of class.
I need a break from books.
It feels great to move around.

We all look forward to it.
It's a chance to unwind.
It's like an escape to freedom.

favorite ('fevərɪt)
wait (wet)
really ('riəlɪ)
get out of
great (gret)
look forward to
unwind (ʌn'waɪnd)
escape (ə'skep)

gym (dʒɪm)
PE ('pi'i)
fun (fʌn)
break (brek)
move around
chance (tʃæns)
like (laɪk)
freedom ('fridəm)

1

We have gym twice a week.

We wear T-shirts and shorts.

We play both inside and out.

PE starts off with exercise.

We stretch, bend and twist.

It's always important to warm up.

We do jumping jacks.

We do push-ups and sit-ups.

Then we jog around the track.

twice〔twaɪs〕

T-shirt〔'ti,ʃɜt〕

inside〔'ɪn'saɪd〕

start off

stretch〔strɛtʃ〕

twist〔twɪst〕

warm〔wɔrm〕

jumping jack

sit-up〔'sɪt,ʌp〕

jog〔dʒɑg〕

wear〔wɛr〕

shorts〔ʃɔrts〕

out〔aʊt〕

exercise〔'ɛksə,saɪz〕

bend〔bɛnd〕

important〔ɪm'pɔrtn̩t〕

warm up

push-up〔'puʃ,ʌp〕

then〔ðɛn〕

track〔træk〕

Finally, the real fun begins.

We divide into teams.

We play sports and compete.

1

I like basketball and dodge ball.

I enjoy badminton and ping-pong, too.

Soccer is the most exciting to me.

Win or lose, it's OK.

There's no pressure at all.

That's why I love gym class so much.

finally ('faɪnḷɪ)	real ('riəl)
fun (fʌn)	divide (də'vaɪd)
team (tim)	play (ple)
sport (sport)	compete (kəm'pit)
dodge (dɑdʒ)	*dodge ball*
badminton ('bædmɪntən)	ping-pong ('pɪŋ,pɑŋ)
soccer ('sɑkɚ)	exciting (ɪk'saɪtɪŋ)
win (wɪn)	lose (luz)
pressure ('prɛʃɚ)	*at all*

1.My Favorite Class

● 演講解說

My favorite class is gym.	我最喜歡的課是體育課。
I can't wait for PE.	我等不及要上體育課。
It's really fun, fun, fun.	體育課眞的非常好玩。
I love to get out of class.	我很喜歡離開教室。
I need a break from books.	我需要離開書本，休息一下。
It feels great to move around.	到處走動的感覺很好。
We all look forward to it.	我們都很期待體育課。
It's a chance to unwind.	那是放鬆一下的機會。
It's like an escape to freedom.	那就像是逃向自由。

✳✳ ─────────────────────

favorite〔'fevərɪt〕*adj.* 最喜歡的　　gym〔dʒɪm〕*n.* 體育
wait〔wet〕*v.* 等待　　PE〔'pi'i〕*n.* 體育（= *physical education*）
really〔'rɪəlɪ〕*adv.* 眞的　　fun〔fʌn〕*adj.* 好玩的；有趣的
get out of 從⋯出來　　break〔brek〕*n.* 休息時間
move around 到處走動　　***look forward to*** 期待
chance〔tʃæns〕*n.* 機會　　unwind〔ʌn'waɪnd〕*v.* 放鬆
like〔laɪk〕*prep.* 像是　　escape〔ə'skep〕*n.* 逃跑；逃跑工具
freedom〔'fridəm〕*n.* 自由

1

We have gym twice a week.	我們一星期上兩堂體育課。
We wear T-shirts and shorts.	我們穿 T 恤和運動褲。
We play both inside and out.	我們會參與室內和室外的體育活動。
PE starts off with exercise.	體育課是從運動開始。
We stretch, bend and twist.	我們會伸展四肢、彎腰和轉動身體。
It's always important to	暖身永遠都很重要。
warm up.	
We do jumping jacks.	我們會做跳躍運動。
We do push-ups and sit-ups.	我們會做伏地挺身和仰臥起坐。
Then we jog around the	然後我們會跑操場。
track.	

**

twice〔twaɪs〕*adv.* 兩次　　wear〔wɛr〕*v.* 穿；戴
T-shirt〔'ti,ʃɜt〕*n.* T 恤；運動衫
shorts〔ʃɔrts〕*n. pl.* 短褲；運動褲　　inside〔'ɪn'saɪd〕*adv.* 在室內
out〔aʊt〕*adv.* 在外面　　*start off* 開始
exercise〔'ɛksə,saɪz〕*n.* 運動　　stretch〔strɛtʃ〕*v.* 伸展肢體
bend〔bɛnd〕*v.* 彎腰　　twist〔twɪst〕*v.* 轉動；轉向
important〔ɪm'pɔrtn̩t〕*adj.* 重要的　　warm〔wɔrm〕*v.* 變溫暖
warm up 做暖身運動　　*jumping jack* 跳躍運動
push-up〔'pʊʃ,ʌp〕*n.* 伏地挺身　　sit-up〔'sɪt,ʌp〕*n.* 仰臥起坐
then〔ðɛn〕*adv.* 然後　　jog〔dʒɑg〕*v.* 慢跑
around〔ə'raʊnd〕*prep.* 繞著　　track〔træk〕*n.*（運動場的）跑道

1

Finally, *the real fun begins*.	最後，真正好玩的事來了。
We divide into teams.	我們會分組。
We play sports and compete.	我們會做一些運動和比賽。
I like basketball and dodge ball.	我喜歡籃球和躲避球。
I enjoy badminton and ping-pong, too.	我還喜歡羽毛球和桌球。
Soccer is the most exciting to me.	對我來說，足球最刺激。
Win or lose, it's OK.	輸贏都沒關係。
There's no pressure at all.	我們沒有任何壓力。
That's why I love gym class so much.	這就是我如此喜愛體育課的原因。

** ────────────────────

finally〔'faɪnlɪ〕*adv.* 最後　　real〔'rɪəl〕*adj.* 真正的
fun〔fʌn〕*n.* 有趣的事　　divide〔də'vaɪd〕*v.* 分開
divide into 分成　　team〔tim〕*n.* 隊；組
play〔ple〕*v.* 參加（體育活動）　　sport〔sport〕*n.* 運動；競賽
compete〔kəm'pit〕*v.* 競爭；比賽　　dodge〔dɑdʒ〕*n.* 躲避
dodge ball 躲避球　　badminton〔'bædmɪntən〕*n.* 羽毛球
ping-pong〔'pɪŋ,pɑŋ〕*n.* 乒乓球；桌球
soccer〔'sɑkɚ〕*n.* 足球　　exciting〔ɪk'saɪtɪŋ〕*adj.* 刺激的
win〔wɪn〕*v.* 贏　　lose〔luz〕*v.* 輸
pressure〔'prɛʃɚ〕*n.* 壓力　　***at all*** 一點也（不）；完全（不）

1

○ 背景說明

　　我們每天都一大早就去上學，每天都上很多不同的
課。在那些課當中，你最期待哪一堂？本篇演講稿，要
教你用英文介紹自己最喜歡的課，讓你一邊學英文，一
邊告訴大家你喜歡那堂課的原因。

1. ***It's really fun, fun, fun.***
   really〔ˈrɪəlɪ〕*adv.* 眞的
   fun〔fʌn〕*adj.* 有趣的；好玩的

　　　　這句話的意思是「體育課
眞的非常好玩。」美國人說話
時，如果要強調某件事，或者是說到情緒激動時，
就會重複講三次，這是美國口語的特色，例如：

　　Hurry, hurry, hurry — you're going to be late!
　　（快、快、快 —— 你快遲到了！）

　　Let's ***win, win, win*** — we have to win!
　　（我們要贏 —— 我們非贏不可！）

　　That was a ***good, good, good*** cup of tea!
　　（這杯茶非常好喝！）

　　That was a ***crazy, crazy, crazy*** thing to do.
　　（做那件事是很瘋狂的。）

　　hurry〔ˈhɝɪ〕*v.* 趕快　　　***be going to V.*** 即將；快要
　　win〔wɪn〕*v.* 贏　　cup〔kʌp〕*n.* 杯子
　　crazy〔ˈkrezɪ〕*adj.* 瘋狂的

1

2. *I love to get out of class.*
   get out of 從…出來

　　　　這句話的字面意思是「我很喜歡從課堂上出來。」
引申爲「我很喜歡離開教室。」也可以說成：

It feels wonderful to leave the classroom.
（離開教室的感覺很棒。）

Getting out of class makes me jump for joy!
（離開教室讓我高興得跳起來！）

leave〔liv〕*v.* 離開
wonderful〔'wʌndɚfəl〕*adj.* 很棒的
jump〔dʒʌmp〕*v.* 跳　　joy〔dʒɔɪ〕*n.* 快樂；高興
jump for joy 高興得跳起來

3. *I need a break from books.*
   need〔nid〕*v.* 需要　　break〔brek〕*n.* 休息時間

　　　　break 的基本意思是「打破」，當動詞用，但在這
裡，是當名詞，作「休息時間」(= *rest*) 解。所以這句
話的意思是「我需要離開書本，休息一下。」也可說成：

I could use some time away from studying.
（我想要一些讀書以外的時間。）

I need to take a rest from my studies.
（我需要放下課業，休息一下。）

could use 想要　　rest〔rɛst〕*n.* 休息
away from 離開　　studies〔'stʌdɪz〕*n. pl.* 讀書；學業

1

4. ***We all look forward to it.***

look forward to 期待

這句話的意思是「我們都
很期待體育課。」也可説成：

We're excited about it.

（體育課讓我們感到很興奮。）

No one can wait for it.

（大家都等不及要上體育課。）

excited〔ɪk'saɪtɪd〕*adj.* 感到興奮的
wait〔wet〕*v.* 等待

look forward to 的用法舉例如下：

I ***look forward to*** Sunday, because I can
  sleep in.

（我很期待星期天，因為可以晚起。）

Most Chinese ***look forward to*** New
  Year's Eve.

（大多數的中國人都很期待除夕夜。）

Children ***look forward to*** receiving gifts.

（孩子們都期待收到禮物。）

Sunday〔'sʌnde〕*n.* 星期天
sleep〔slip〕*v.* 睡覺　　***sleep in*** 晚起；睡過頭
Chinese〔tʃaɪ'niz〕*n. pl.* 中國人
eve〔iv〕*n.* 前夕　　***New Year's Eve*** 除夕夜
receive〔rɪ'siv〕*v.* 收到　　gift〔gɪft〕*n.* 禮物

1

5. *It's a chance to unwind.*

chance〔tʃæns〕*n.* 機會　　unwind〔ʌn'waɪnd〕*v.* 放鬆

wind 有兩種唸法，作「風」解時，是名詞，唸成〔wɪnd〕，而作「上緊（發條）；纏繞」解時，是動詞，唸成〔waɪnd〕，在本句中的 unwind 是「上緊（發條）」的相反詞，作「放鬆」解，所以要唸成〔ʌn'waɪnd〕。

這句話的意思是「那是放鬆一下的機會。」也可說成：

It's a chance to take a break.
（那是休息一下的機會。）
It's an opportunity to relax.
（那是放鬆一下的機會。）

break〔brek〕*n.* 休息時間
take a break 休息一下
opportunity〔ˌɑpə'tjunətɪ〕*n.* 機會
relax〔rɪ'læks〕*v.* 放鬆

6. *It's like an escape to freedom.*

like〔laɪk〕*prep.* 像是
escape〔ə'skep〕*n.* 逃跑；逃跑工具
freedom〔'fridəm〕*n.* 自由

escape 的基本意思是「逃跑」，當動詞用，但在這裡，是當名詞用，所以這句話的意思是「那就像是逃向自由。」也可說成：It's a way to get free.（那是獲得自由的方式。）

【way〔we〕*n.* 方式　　free〔fri〕*adj.* 自由的】

7. ***We play both inside and out.***

play〔ple〕*v.* 參與（體育活動）

inside〔'ɪn'saɪd〕*adv.* 在室內　　out〔aʊt〕*adv.* 在外面

　　　　play 的基本意思是「玩」，但在這裡是引申作「參與（體育活動）」解，所以這句話的意思是「我們會參與室內和室外的體育活動。」也可說成：

　　We have PE in the gym or out on the
　　　　sports field.

　　（我們會在體育館或是運動場上體育課。）

　　Sometimes we compete inside,
　　　　sometimes outside.

　　（我們有時候會在室內比賽，有時候在室外。）

　　PE〔'pi'i〕*n.* 體育　　gym〔dʒɪm〕*n.* 體育館
　　field〔fild〕*n.* 場；用地
　　compete〔kəm'pit〕*v.* 競爭；比賽
　　outside〔'aʊt'saɪd〕*adv.* 在外面

8. ***We do jumping jacks.***

jumping jack 跳躍運動

　　　　jumping jack 這個詞是源自一百多年前的英國，指的是一種用線控制的木偶，只要拉動線，木偶就會跳來跳去。後來，這個字就引申作「跳躍運動」。

　　　　專家說跳躍運動有助於小孩子的骨骼發育，它的動作就是跳起後，雙腿張開，雙手高舉過頭，在一般的體操中，都會出現這樣的動作。

1

9. ***Then we jog around the track.***

then〔ðɛn〕*adv.* 然後　　jog〔dʒɑg〕*v.* 慢跑
around〔ə'raund〕*prep.* 繞著　　track〔træk〕*n.* 跑道

這句話的意思是「然後我們會跑操場。」在本句中，track 是當名詞，作「(運動場的) 跑道」解，所以這句話也可說成：Then we jog around the schoolyard. (然後我們會繞著運動場跑。)

【schoolyard〔'skul͵jɑrd〕*n.* 校園；運動場】

另外，track 還可以當動詞用，作「追蹤」解，例如：They ***tracked*** the plane by radar. (他們用雷達來追蹤那架飛機。)

【plane〔plen〕*n.* 飛機　　radar〔'redɑr〕*n.* 雷達】

10. ***Win or lose, it's OK.***

win〔wɪn〕*v.* 贏　　lose〔luz〕*v.* 輸
OK〔'o'ke〕*adj.* 好的；可以的 (= *okay*)

這句話的字面意思是「贏或輸都好。」也就是「輸贏都沒關係。」還可說成：

We don't mind if we win or lose.
(我們不介意輸贏。)
We play for fun, not to win.
(我們是爲了好玩而比賽，不是爲了要贏。)
It doesn't matter whether we win or lose.
(我們是贏還是輸，並不重要。)

mind〔maind〕*v.* 介意　　matter〔'mætɚ〕*v.* 關係重要
whether〔'hwɛðɚ〕*conj.* 不論

○ 作文範例

My Favorite Class

My favorite class at school is PE class. We have it twice a week in the afternoons. I really look forward to it, because after several hours of studying hard, I need a break from the books. *Therefore*, I can't wait to get out of the classroom and head for the gym.

We always start off with stretching because it's important to warm up. Then we do some jumping jacks and other exercises before jogging around the track. After that the real fun begins. We divide up into teams and compete at different sports. Basketball and dodge ball are my favorite games. There's no pressure to win. We just have fun while strengthening our bodies. That's why I like PE class so much.

● 中文翻譯

我最喜歡的課程

　　我在學校最喜歡的課是體育課。我們每個星期都有兩個下午要上體育課。我真的很期待上體育課，因為在努力唸了幾個小時的書之後，我需要離開書本休息一下。因此，我等不及要走出教室，然後走向體育館。

　　我們總是從伸展四肢開始，因為暖身很重要。然後在跑操場之前，我們會做一些跳躍運動和其他的運動。做完那些之後，真正好玩的事來了。我們會分組，然後在不同的比賽中競爭。籃球和躲避球是我最喜歡的運動。我們沒有要贏的壓力。我們只是一邊使身體變強壯，一邊玩樂。那就是我這麼麼喜歡體育課的原因。

2. My Favorite Holiday

My favorite holiday is New Year.
Westerners call it Chinese New Year.
We call it Lunar New Year.

It's a big celebration.
It's an important festival.
It's the highlight of the year.

New Year comes during winter.
It's cold and chilly then.
But our hearts are warm and cheerful.

2

favorite ('fevərɪt)
holiday ('halə,de)
call (kɔl)
celebration (,sɛlə'breʃən)
festival ('fɛstəvl̩)
chilly ('tʃɪlɪ)
heart (hart)
cheerful ('tʃɪrfəl)

Westerner ('wɛstənə)
lunar ('lunə)
important (ɪm'pɔrtn̩t)
highlight ('haɪ'laɪt)
then (ðɛn)
warm (wɔrm)

2

We follow old customs.

We stick red couplets beside our doors.

We clean up and sweep out our houses.

Everyone returns home.

Families get together.

We chat and have a big feast.

People visit each other.

We greet relatives and neighbors.

We exchange best wishes and gifts.

follow (ˈfɑlo)	custom (ˈkʌstəm)
stick (stɪk)	couplet (ˈkʌplɪt)
beside (bɪˈsaɪd)	*clean up*
sweep (swip)	return (rɪˈtɜn)
get together	chat (tʃæt)
feast (fist)	visit (ˈvɪzɪt)
greet (grit)	relative (ˈrɛlətɪv)
neighbor (ˈnebɚ)	exchange (ɪksˈtʃendʒ)
wish (wɪʃ)	gift (gɪft)

It's a super time for kids.

We get presents and treats.

We set off fireworks, too.

2

Best of all are red envelopes.

They're gifts of money.

We all love them the most.

New Year is a time to give thanks.

We're grateful and happy.

We expect a great year ahead.

super ('supɚ)   kid (kɪd)

present ('prɛznt)   treat (trit)

set off   firework ('faɪr‚wɝk)

envelope ('ɛnvə‚lop)   gift (gɪft)

thank (θæŋk)   grateful ('gretfəl)

expect (ɪk'spɛkt)   great (gret)

ahead (ə'hɛd)

2. My Favorite Holiday

○ 演講解說

2

My favorite holiday is New Year.　　　我最喜歡的節日是新年。
Westerners call it Chinese New　　　西方人稱之為中國新年。
　　Year.
We call it Lunar New Year.　　　我們把它叫作農曆新年。

It's a big celebration.　　　那是個盛大的慶典。
It's an important festival.　　　那是很重要的節日。
It's the highlight of the year.　　　那是一年之中最重要的日子。

New Year comes during winter.　　　新年會在冬天的時候來臨。
It's cold and chilly then.　　　那時會非常冷。
But our hearts are warm and　　　但是我們的心卻又暖又愉快。
　　cheerful.

** ——————————————

favorite〔ˈfevərɪt〕*adj.* 最喜歡的　　Westerner〔ˈwɛstənə〕*n.* 西方人
call〔kɔl〕*v.* 稱為；叫作　　lunar〔ˈlunə〕*adj.* 陰曆的
celebration〔ˌsɛləˈbreʃən〕*n.* 慶典；慶祝活動
important〔ɪmˈpɔrtn̩t〕*adj.* 重要的　　festival〔ˈfɛstəvl̩〕*n.* 節日；慶典
highlight〔ˈhaɪˈlaɪt〕*n.* 最重要的部分　　chilly〔ˈtʃɪlɪ〕*adj.* 很冷的
then〔ðɛn〕*adv.* 那時　　heart〔hɑrt〕*n.* 心
warm〔wɔrm〕*adj.* 溫暖的　　cheerful〔ˈtʃɪrfəl〕*adj.* 愉快的

We follow old customs.　　　　　　我們會遵照古老的習俗。

We stick red couplets beside　　　我們會在門旁邊貼紅色的
　　our doors.　　　　　　　　　　　春聯。

We clean up and sweep out our　　我們會清理並打掃房子。
　　houses.

Everyone returns home.　　　　　　每個人都會回家。

Families get together.　　　　　　　家人會團聚在一起。

We chat and have a big feast.　　　我們會聊天，還有吃大餐。

People visit each other.　　　　　　人們會互相拜訪。

We greet relatives and neighbors.　我們會問候親戚和鄰居。

We exchange best wishes and　　　我們會互相給予誠摯的祝
　　gifts.　　　　　　　　　　　　福，並送禮給對方。

**　──────────────────────

follow〔ˋfɑlo〕*v.* 遵照　　　custom〔ˋkʌstəm〕*n.* 習俗

stick〔stɪk〕*v.* 貼上　　　couplet〔ˋkʌplɪt〕*n.* 對句

beside〔bɪˋsaɪd〕*prep.* 在⋯的旁邊　***clean up*** 清掃乾淨

sweep〔swip〕*v.* 打掃　　***sweep out*** 打掃

return〔rɪˋtɜn〕*v.* 返回　　***get together*** 相聚

chat〔tʃæt〕*v.* 聊天　　feast〔fist〕*n.* 豐富的大餐；盛宴

visit〔ˋvɪzɪt〕*v.* 拜訪　　greet〔grit〕*v.* 和～打招呼；問候

relative〔ˋrɛlətɪv〕*n.* 親戚　　neighbor〔ˋnebɚ〕*n.* 鄰居

exchange〔ɪksˋtʃendʒ〕*v.* 交換；互相（問候等）

wish〔wɪʃ〕*n.* 祝福　　gift〔gɪft〕*n.* 禮物

It's a super time for kids.	那是小孩子最快樂的時光。
We get presents and treats.	我們會拿到禮物，並享用美食。
We set off fireworks, too.	我們還會放煙火。
Best of all are red envelopes.	最棒的是紅包。
They're gifts of money.	它們是一種禮金。
We all love them the most.	我們都最喜歡紅包。
New Year is a time to give thanks.	新年是表達感謝的時刻。
We're grateful and happy.	我們都滿懷感激，而且非常開心。
We expect a great year ahead.	我們期待明年會過得很好。

2

** ————————————————

super〔'supɚ〕*adj.* 極好的　　kid〔kɪd〕*n.* 小孩
present〔'prɛzn̩t〕*n.* 禮物
treat〔trit〕*n.* 非常好的事物；美食
set off 燃放　　firework〔'faɪr͵wɝk〕*n.* 煙火
envelope〔'ɛnvə͵lop〕*n.* 信封　　gift〔gɪft〕*n.* 禮物
thank〔θæŋk〕*n.* 感謝　　grateful〔'gretfəl〕*adj.* 感激的
expect〔ɪk'spɛkt〕*v.* 期待　　great〔gret〕*adj.* 很棒的
ahead〔ə'hɛd〕*adv.* 往後；將來

● 背景說明

　　中國人有許多大大小小的節日，每個節日都有它的特色，新年可以拿紅包，端午節有粽子吃，中秋節可以烤肉。在這些節日當中，你最喜歡哪一個呢？我們一起來練習用英文介紹你最喜歡的節日吧！

1. *Westerners call it Chinese New Year.*
   Westerner〔'wɛstənə〕*n.* 西方人
   call〔kɔl〕*v.* 稱為；叫作

　　這句話的意思是「西方人稱之為中國新年。」

　　call 的主要意思是「呼叫」，但在這裡，引申作「稱為；叫作」解，要特別注意的是，此時 call 是「不完全及物動詞」，後面除了要有受詞（it），還要有受詞補語（Chinese New Year），這樣句意才會完整，例如：

　　The teacher ***called*** <u>the student</u> <u>a lazybones</u>.
　　　　　　　　　　　　 受　詞　　　　 受詞補語
　　（老師叫那位學生懶鬼。）

　　He ***called*** <u>me</u> <u>fat</u>.（他叫我胖子。）
　　　　　　　 受詞 受詞補語

　　lazybones〔'lezɪ,bonz〕*n.* 懶骨頭；懶鬼
　　fat〔fæt〕*n.* 肥肉；胖子

2. *We call it Lunar New Year.*

lunar〔'lunɚ〕*adj.* 陰曆的

這句話的意思是「我們把它叫作農曆新年。」lunar 原本的意思是「月亮的」，在此引申作「陰曆的」解，例如：lunar calendar（陰曆），而「陽曆」則是 solar calendar。

【solar〔'solɚ〕*adj.* 陽曆的；太陽的】

3. *It's the highlight of the year.*

highlight〔'haɪ'laɪt〕*n.* 最重要的部分

highlight 的基本意思是「給予強光」，在此引申為「最重要的部分」，所以這句話的意思是「那是一年之中最重要的日子。」也可說成：It's the most important part of the year.（那是一年之中最重要的部分。）

【important〔ɪm'pɔrtn̩t〕*adj.* 重要的　part〔pɑrt〕*n.* 部分】

highlight 的用法舉例如下：

The weekend is the *highlight* of my week.
（週末是我一星期中最重要的部分。）

Summer vacation is a *highlight* for
　most students.
（對大多數的學生來說，暑假是最重要的部分。）

weekend〔'wik'ɛnd〕*n.* 週末　summer〔'sʌmɚ〕*adj.* 夏天的
vacation〔ve'keʃən〕*n.* 假期　　*summer vacation* 暑假

2

4. *We follow old customs.*

follow〔'falo〕*v.* 遵照　　custom〔'kʌstəm〕*n.* 習俗

　　　follow 原本的意思是「跟隨」，在此引申作「遵照」(=*obey*)解，所以這句話的意思是「我們會遵照古老的習俗。」也可以説成：

　　　We act according to tradition.
　　　（我們根據傳統來行事。）

　　　We stick to the old ways of doing things.
　　　（我們遵守古老的方法來做事。）

　　　according to 根據　　tradition〔trə'dıʃən〕*n.* 傳統
　　　stick〔stık〕*v.* 遵守　　***stick to*** 遵守
　　　way〔we〕*n.* 方法

5. *We stick red couplets beside our doors.*

stick〔stık〕*v.* 貼上　　couplet〔'kʌplıt〕*n.* 對句
beside〔bı'saıd〕*prep.* 在…的旁邊

　　　這句話的意思是「我們會在門旁邊貼紅色的春聯。」couplet 本身是「對句」的意思，而 red couplet 就是中國人所説的「春聯」。

　　　傳説春聯是由「桃符」演變而來的，而桃符是古代畫上門神的木板。五代時，孟昶心血來潮，在桃符上提了兩句對句，於是就演變成了現在的春聯。

2

6. *Families get together*.

family〔'fæməlɪ〕 *n.* 家人　　*get together* 相聚

　　這句話的意思是「家人會團聚在一起。」也可說成：

Families reunite.
（家人會團圓。）

Family members return home.
（家族成員會回家。）

Families meet and gather together.
（家人會見個面，然後聚一聚。）

reunite〔ˌrijʊ'naɪt〕 *v.* 團圓；重聚
member〔'mɛmbɚ〕 *n.* 成員　　return〔rɪ'tɝn〕 *v.* 返回
meet〔mit〕 *v.* 見面　　gather〔'gæðɚ〕 *v.* 聚集
together〔tə'gɛðɚ〕 *adv.* 一起

　　另外，get together 是作「相聚」解，是動詞片語，但是如果中間多一橫，變成 "get-together"，則是名詞，作「聚會；會議」解，例如：

Do you think we can *get together* at
　　Christmas?（你想我們能在聖誕節相聚嗎？）
【*get together* 是動詞】

Most weddings are big family *get-togethers*.
（大多數的婚禮，都是大家族的聚會時間。）
【*get-together* 是名詞】

Christmas〔'krɪsməs〕 *n.* 聖誕節
wedding〔'wɛdɪŋ〕 *n.* 婚禮

7. *We greet relatives and neighbors.*

greet〔grit〕*v.* 和～打招呼；問候
relative〔'rɛlətɪv〕*n.* 親戚　　neighbor〔'nebɚ〕*n.* 鄰居

2

這句話的意思是「我們會問候親戚和鄰居。」也可說成：We say hello to everyone we know.（我們會跟每個認識的人打招呼。）

greet 是「和～打招呼；問候」的意思，例如：

A warm smile is the best way to ***greet*** people.
（跟別人打招呼的最佳方式，就是親切的微笑。）

She ***greeted*** her teacher politely.
（她很有禮貌地跟老師打招呼。）

warm〔wɔrm〕*adj.* 親切的
politely〔pə'laɪtlɪ〕*adv.* 有禮貌地

8. *We get presents and treats.*

present〔'prɛznt〕*n.* 禮物
treat〔trit〕*n.* 非常好的事物；美食

treat 的基本意思是「對待」，但在這裡，是當名詞用，作「非常好的事物」解，引申為「美食」。所以這句話的意思是「我們會拿到禮物，並享用美食。」也可說成：

We receive gifts and candy.
（我們會收到禮物和糖果。）

People give us nice things and yummy snacks.
（人們會給我們好東西，還有好吃的點心。）

receive〔rɪ'siv〕*v.* 收到　　gift〔gɪft〕*n.* 禮物
yummy〔'jʌmɪ〕*adj.* 好吃的　　snack〔snæk〕*n.* 點心

9. **We set off fireworks, too.**

　　set off 燃放　　firework〔ˈfaɪrˌwɜk〕n. 煙火

　　　　set off 在此是作「燃放」(= light) 解，所以這句話的意思是「我們還會放煙火。」也可說成：

　　　　　　We launch rockets into the sky.
　　　　　　（我們對著天空發射煙火。）

　　　　　　We shoot off fireworks into the sky.
　　　　　　（我們對著天空放煙火。）

　　　　launch〔lɔntʃ〕v. 發射　　rocket〔ˈrɑkɪt〕n. 煙火
　　　　sky〔skaɪ〕n. 天空　　shoot〔ʃut〕v. 發射
　　　　shoot off 對空燃放（煙火）

　　　　set off 有很多種意思，必須依前後句意來判斷，下面是主要的意思：

① 作「燃放；使爆炸」解。
　　The soldier stepped on a wire which **set off** a bomb.（那名士兵踩到了使炸彈爆炸的電線。）

② 作「出發」(= depart) 解。
　　I **set off** for school at 7:30 every morning.
　　（我每天早上七點半出發去上學。）

③ 作「引發」解。
　　The earthquake **set off** a wave of panic.
　　（這次地震引發一陣恐慌。）

　step〔stɛp〕v. 踩　　wire〔waɪr〕n. 電線
　bomb〔bɑm〕n. 炸彈　　earthquake〔ˈɜθˌkwek〕n. 地震
　wave〔wev〕n.（情緒等的）起伏；高漲
　a wave of 一陣　　panic〔ˈpænɪk〕n. 恐慌

○作文範例

My Favorite Holiday

My favorite holiday is New Year. It's a very important festival in Chinese culture. *In fact*, it's the highlight of the year. Everyone returns home for a family reunion. We have a big feast and chat about all the things that have happened in our lives. People also visit each other. We exchange gifts and good wishes for the next year.

New Year is especially fun for kids. That's because we get presents and treats, including red envelopes filled with money. We also get to set off fireworks. But we never forget that this holiday is a time to give thanks. We feel grateful for our family and the things that we have. *Finally*, we think about the future and the great year ahead.

● 中文翻譯

我最喜歡的節日

　　我最喜歡的節日是新年。在中國文化中，那是個很重要的節慶。事實上，那是一年之中最重要的日子。每個人都會回家跟家人團聚。我們會吃頓大餐，然後聊聊生活中所發生的一切。人們也會互相拜訪。我們會互相送禮，並祝福對方明年過得更好。

　　新年對小孩子來說特別好玩。那是因為我們會得到禮物和美食，包括裝滿錢的紅包。我們還能放煙火。但是我們絕不會忘記，這個節日是表達感謝的時刻。我們會對家人，還有自己所擁有的東西滿懷感激。最後，我們會想想未來，並希望明年過得很好。

3. My Summer Vacation

Hurray for July!
Three cheers for August!
I love the summertime.

3

No school for two months.
No worrying about tests.
And a lot less homework to do.

I get to do what I want.
I'm as free as a bird.
It's my dream come true.

---

summer ('sʌmɚ)
hurray (hə're)
cheer (tʃɪr)
August ('ɔgəst)
month (mʌnθ)
a lot
homework ('hom,wɝk)
free (fri)

vacation (ve'keʃən)
July (dʒu'laɪ)
three cheers for
summertime ('sʌmɚ,taɪm)
worry ('wɝɪ)
less (lɛs)
get to
dream come true

3

***Summer is a chance to relax*.**

I read interesting books.

I watch my favorite TV programs.

I hang out with my friends.

We roam around the neighborhood.

We enjoy staying up late.

I visit my grandparents.

I travel with my family.

We take fun trips all around.

chance〔tʃæns〕

interesting〔'ɪntrɪstɪŋ〕

program〔'progræm〕

roam〔rom〕

neighborhood〔'nebɚ,hʊd〕

late〔let〕

grandparents〔'græn,pɛrənts〕

travel〔'trævl̩〕

fun〔fʌn〕

all around

relax〔rɪ'læks〕

favorite〔'fevərɪt〕

hang out with

around〔ə'raʊnd〕

stay up

visit〔'vɪzɪt〕

take〔tek〕

trip〔trɪp〕

***Summer is a time to learn more*.**

I try to improve my weak areas.

I try to learn something new.

Last summer, I took swimming lessons.

This summer, I might join a sports camp.

Maybe I'll study computers or English.

Remember summer days fly by fast.

The vacation is over too soon.

So do as much as you can.

---

try (traɪ)

weak (wik)

last (læst)

swimming ('swɪmɪŋ)

join (dʒɔɪn)

camp (kæmp).

computer (kəm'pjutɚ)

fly (flaɪ)

fast (fæst)

soon (sun)

improve (ɪm'pruv)

area ('ɛrɪə)

take (tek)

lesson ('lɛsn̩)

sports (sports)

maybe ('mebi)

remember (rɪ'mɛmbɚ)

fly by

over ('ovɚ)

as···as one can

3. My Summer Vacation

● 演講解說

Hurray for July!	七月萬歲！
Three cheers for August!	爲八月歡呼三聲吧！
I love the summertime.	我愛夏天。
No school for two months.	有兩個月不用上學。
No worrying about tests.	不用擔心考試。
And a lot less homework to do.	而且要做的家庭作業也少很多。
I get to do what I want.	我可以做自己想做的事。
I'm as free as a bird.	我會像鳥兒一樣自由。
It's my dream come true.	我的美夢成眞。

** ———

summer〔'sʌmɚ〕*adj.* 夏天的　　vacation〔ve'keʃən〕*n.* 假期
hurray〔hə're〕*interj.* 萬歲！　　July〔dʒu'laɪ〕*n.* 七月
cheer〔tʃɪr〕*n.* 歡呼；萬歲　　*three cheers for* 爲…歡呼三聲
August〔'ɔgəst〕*n.* 八月　　summertime〔'sʌmɚ͵taɪm〕*n.* 夏天
school〔skul〕*n.* 上學　　month〔mʌnθ〕*n.* 月
worry〔'wɝɪ〕*v.* 擔心　　*a lot*【當副詞用】…得多；大大地
less〔lɛs〕*adj.* 較少的　　homework〔'hom͵wɝk〕*n.* 家庭作業
get to 得以；能夠　　free〔fri〕*adj.* 自由的
dream〔drim〕*n.* 夢想　　*dream come true* 夢想成眞

Summer is a chance to relax.	夏天是放鬆的好機會。
I read interesting books.	我會讀有趣的書。
I watch my favorite TV programs.	我會看我最喜歡的電視節目。
I hang out with my friends.	我會和朋友在一起。
We roam around the neighborhood.	我們會在附近閒逛。
We enjoy staying up late.	我們喜歡熬夜。
I visit my grandparents.	我會去探望祖父母。
I travel with my family.	我會和家人去旅遊。
We take fun trips all around.	我會到處從事有趣的旅行。

3

**

summer〔ˈsʌmɚ〕*n.* 夏天　　chance〔tʃæns〕*n.* 機會
relax〔rɪˈlæks〕*v.* 放鬆　　interesting〔ˈɪntrɪstɪŋ〕*adj.* 有趣的
favorite〔ˈfevərɪt〕*adj.* 最喜歡的
program〔ˈprogræm〕*n.* 節目　　***hang out with*** 和⋯在一起
roam〔rom〕*v.* 閒逛　　around〔əˈraʊnd〕*prep.* 在⋯附近
neighborhood〔ˈnebɚˌhʊd〕*n.* 鄰近地區　　***stay up*** 熬夜
late〔let〕*adv.* 到很晚；到深夜　　visit〔ˈvɪzɪt〕*v.* 拜訪；探望
grandparents〔ˈgrænˌpɛrənts〕*n. pl.* 祖父母
travel〔ˈtrævl̩〕*v.* 旅行　　take〔tek〕*v.* 做
fun〔fʌn〕*adj.* 有趣的；好玩的　　trip〔trɪp〕*n.* 旅行
take a trip 去旅行　　***all around*** 到處

3

Summer is a time to learn more.　夏天是多學一點東西的時間。

I try to improve my weak areas.　我要努力改善比較弱的地方。

I try to learn something new.　我要努力學習新東西。

Last summer, I took swimming lessons.　去年夏天，我去上了游泳課。

This summer, I might join a sports camp.　今年夏天，我可能會參加運動營。

Maybe I'll study computers or English.　也許我會去學電腦或英文。

Remember summer days fly by fast.　切記，夏天稍縱即逝。

The vacation is over too soon.　假期很快就結束。

So do as much as you can.　所以要盡你所能去做。

※※ ——————————————

try〔traɪ〕*v.* 努力；試圖　improve〔ɪm'pruv〕*v.* 改善

weak〔wik〕*adj.* 虛弱的；不佳的　area〔'ɛrɪə〕*n.* 地方；領域

last〔læst〕*adj.* 上一個的　take〔tek〕*v.* 上（課）

swimming〔'swɪmɪŋ〕*adj.* 游泳的　lesson〔'lɛsn̩〕*n.* 課程

join〔dʒɔɪn〕*v.* 參加　sports〔sports〕*adj.* 運動的

camp〔kæmp〕*n.* 營隊　computer〔kəm'pjutɚ〕*n.* 電腦

remember〔rɪ'mɛmbɚ〕*v.* 記住

fly〔flaɪ〕*v.* （時間）飛也似地過去　***fly by*** 時間（飛逝）

fast〔fæst〕*adv.* 快速地　over〔'ovɚ〕*adv.* 結束

soon〔sun〕*adv.* 很快　***as…as one can*** 盡其所能

● 背景說明

　　每年的暑假，你都在做什麼呢？平常沒時間做的事，或是無法實現的夢想，通通可以利用這兩個月的時間來實現！在暑假裡，你可以盡情玩樂，盡情看電視，學你想學的才藝，讀你想讀的書，無論如何，千萬不要白白浪費時間喔！

3

1. *Hurray for July!*

hurray〔 hə'reɪ 〕*interj.* 萬歲！
July〔 dʒu'laɪ 〕*n.* 七月

　　當老師宣布明天開始放暑假時，你就可以説：Hurray for July! 意思是「七月萬歲！」，也可以説：Cheers for July!（為七月歡呼！）【cheer〔 tʃɪr 〕*n.* 歡呼】

Hurray 在此是當感嘆詞用，例如：

Hurray for the Queen!（女王萬歲！）

Hurray! We're getting an extra day off.
（萬歲！我們可以多放一天假了。）

Hurray! Our team has won!
（萬歲！我們這一隊贏了！）

queen〔 kwin 〕*n.* 女王；皇后
extra〔'ɛkstrə〕*adj.* 額外的　　off〔 ɔf 〕*adv.* 休假
team〔 tim 〕*n.* 隊伍　　win〔 wɪn 〕*v.* 贏

3

2. ***Three cheers for August!***

cheer〔tʃɪr〕*n.* 歡呼；萬歲
three cheers for 為⋯歡呼三聲　　August〔ˈɔgəst〕*n.* 八月

　　這句話的意思是「為八月歡呼三聲吧！」美國人要歡呼三聲時，會有一個人先帶頭喊 "Hip, hip!"，然後所有人再一起喊 "Hurray!" 三次。和中國古代見到皇帝時，說的：「萬歲！萬歲！萬萬歲！」有異曲同工之妙。【hip〔hɪp〕*interj.* 歡呼的聲音】

這句話也可說成：

　　　Hurray for August!（八月萬歲！）

　　　Thank God for August!

　　　（感謝上帝，八月到了！）

　　　August is the best!（八月最棒了！）

另外，cheer 的用法舉例如下：

　① 當名詞用，作「歡呼；萬歲」解。
　　Three ***cheers*** for the winner!
　　（為優勝者歡呼三聲！）

　② 當動詞用，作「振作」解。
　　Cheer up!（振作精神！）

　③ 當感嘆詞用，作「乾杯」解。
　　"***Cheers***," he said. "To your health!"
　　（「乾杯！」他說。「祝你健康!」）

　　【winner〔ˈwɪnɚ〕*n.* 贏家；優勝者　　health〔hɛlθ〕*n.* 健康】

3. *And a lot less homework to do.*

a lot　【當副詞用】…得多；大大地

less〔lɛs〕*adj.* 較少的

homework〔'hom,wɝk〕*n.* 家庭作業

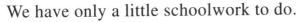

這句話的意思是「而且要做的家庭作業也少很多。」也可説成：

Not much homework to do.

（要寫的家庭作業不多。）

We have only a little schoolwork to do.

（我們只有一點點功課要寫。）

【schoolwork〔'skul,wɝk〕*n.* 功課】

我們很常看到 a lot 當形容詞用，例如：There are *a lot* of parks in Taiwan.（台灣有很多公園。）但在這裡，a lot 是當副詞用，例如：

You've changed *a lot*.（你變了很多。）

A lot fewer people smoke cigarettes now.

（現在抽煙的人少很多了。）

There are *a lot* more Starbucks in Taiwan right now.

（現在，台灣多了很多星巴客。）

change〔tʃendʒ〕*v.* 改變

fewer〔'fjuɚ〕*adj.* 較少的　　smoke〔smok〕*v.* 抽煙

cigarette〔,sɪgə'rɛt , 'sɪgə,rɛt〕*n.* 香煙

right now 現在

4. *I get to do what I want.*

　　get to 得以；能夠

　　　　get 的意思是「得到」，而 get to 的意思是「得以；能夠」（= *can*），所以本句的意思是「我可以做自己想做的事。」也可說成：I can do anything.（我可以做任何事。）

5. *I'm as free as a bird.*

　　as⋯***as***～　和～一樣⋯　　free〔fri〕*adj.* 自由的

　　　　這句話的意思是「我會像鳥兒一樣自由。」也可說成：I'm totally free.（我完全自由。）
【totally〔'totḷɪ〕*adv.* 完全地】

　　　　as⋯***as***～是「和～一樣⋯」的意思，以下都是美國人常用的比喻，非常有趣：

I'm ***as*** happy ***as*** a lark.
（我像雲雀一樣快樂；我非常快樂。）

He's ***as*** stubborn ***as*** a mule.
（他像騾子一樣固執；他非常頑固。）

She is ***as*** sly ***as*** a fox.
（她像狐狸一樣狡猾；她非常狡猾。）

My dad is ***as*** strong ***as*** an ox.（我爸壯得像條牛。）

lark〔lɑrk〕*n.* 雲雀　　　stubborn〔'stʌbɚn〕*adj.* 固執的
mule〔mjul〕*n.* 騾子　　　sly〔slaɪ〕*adj.* 狡猾的
fox〔fɑks〕*n.* 狐狸　　　　strong〔strɔŋ〕*adj.* 強壯的
ox〔ɑks〕*n.* 公牛

3

6. *It's my dream come true.*

dream〔drim〕*n.* 夢想　　***dream come true*** 夢想成眞

　　這句話的意思是「我的美夢成眞。」my dream come true 是固定用法，和 a dream come true 相同，是名詞片語，可能來自 a dream that comes true 或 a dream coming true。【註：固定用法即慣用語，沒有文法可言，美國人就是習慣這樣說。】

7. *This summer, I might join a sports camp.*

join〔dʒɔɪn〕*v.* 參加　　sports〔sports〕*adj.* 運動的
camp〔kæmp〕*n.* 營隊

　　這句話的意思是「今年夏天，我可能會參加運動營。」在台灣，暑假的時候，學生們很流行參加夏令營（summer camp），或是英語訓練營（English camp），但在國外，他們最流行的，就是參加運動營（sports camp），幾乎每一所大學或高中，都會舉辦這樣的活動。

這句話也可以說成：

　　I'm thinking about attending a sports camp
　　　this summer.（今年夏天，我考慮要參加運動營。）

　　I want to go to a basketball camp this summer.
　　（我今年夏天想要參加籃球營。）

　　attend〔əˈtɛnd〕*v.* 參加
　　basketball〔ˈbæskɪtˌbɔl〕*n.* 籃球

3

8. *Remember summer days fly by fast.*

remember〔rɪˋmɛmbɚ〕v. 記得
fly〔flaɪ〕v.（時間）飛也似地過去　　*fly by* 時間（飛逝）
fast〔fæst〕adv. 快速地

　　fly 的主要意思是「飛」，當前面的主詞是時間時，fly 就有時光飛逝的意思，所以這句話要翻成「切記，夏天稍縱即逝。」也可說成：

Don't forget summer days pass quickly.
（別忘了，夏天過得很快。）

Keep in mind that summer goes by quickly.
（記住，夏天過得很快。）

forget〔fɚˋgɛt〕v. 忘記　　pass〔pæs〕v. 過去
quickly〔ˋkwɪklɪ〕adv. 快速地
keep in mind 記住　　*go by* 過去

9. *So do as much as you can.*

as⋯as one can 盡其所能

　　這句話的意思是「所以要盡你所能去做。」as⋯as *one* can 是作「盡其所能」（= *as⋯as possible*）解，如：

At buffets, I try to eat *as* much *as I can*.
（吃歐式自助餐時，我會盡我所能地努力吃。）

While in school, always learn *as* much *as you can*.（在學校的時候，一定要盡你所能地學習。）

buffet〔bʌˋfe〕n. 歐式自助餐
while〔hwaɪl〕conj. 當⋯的時候

● 作文範例

My Summer Vacation

Summertime is the best time of the year. There is no school for two months and I get to do what I want. With no tests and no homework, I'm as free as a bird.

3

I do many things during the summer vacation. I relax by reading books and watching TV. I also hang out with my friends and travel with my family. *However,* I don't only play in summer. I take advantage of the free time to learn more. *For example,* last summer I learned to swim. This summer I might study computers or English. Summer vacation flies by fast, so it's important to do as much as you can.

3

● 中文翻譯

我 的 暑 假

　　夏天是一年之中最棒的時間。有兩個月不用上學,所以我可以做我想做的事。沒有考試,沒有家庭作業,我就像鳥兒一樣自由。

　　我會在暑假期間做很多事。我會看看書和電視,來放鬆一下。我還會和朋友在一起,然後跟家人去旅行。但是在夏天時,我不會只顧著玩。我會利用空閒時間來多學一點東西。例如,去年暑假我學會了游泳。今年暑假,我可能會學電腦或英文。暑假稍縱即逝,所以盡你所能去做是很重要的。

4. My Grandparents

My grandparents are so sweet.
They hold a special place in my heart.
They're more precious than gold.

They worked hard all their lives.
They sacrificed for my family.
They raised my parents very well.

4

I owe them thanks and praise.
I'm alive because of them.
I don't know how to repay them.

grandparents (ˈɡrænˌpɛrənts)
hold (hold)
place (ples)
precious (ˈprɛʃəs)
hard (hɑrd)
sacrifice (ˈsækrəˌfaɪs)
parents (ˈpɛrənts)
thank (θæŋk)
alive (əˈlaɪv)

sweet (swit)
special (ˈspɛʃəl)
heart (hɑrt)
gold (gold)
all one's life
raise (rez)
owe (o)
praise (prez)
repay (rɪˈpe)

4

My grandparents are special friends.
They're easygoing and understanding.
They're easier to talk to than my parents.

My grandma makes me delicious foods.
My grandpa takes me fishing and
    kite-flying.
They are wonderful babysitters and
    companions.

They are full of wisdom, too.
They explain right and wrong.
They teach me to be honest and fair.

easygoing (ˈizɪˈgoɪŋ)
understanding (ˌʌndɚˈstændɪŋ)
talk (tɔk)   grandma (ˈgrænma)
make (mek)   delicious (dɪˈlɪʃəs)
grandpa (ˈgrænpa)   take (tek)
fishing (ˈfɪʃɪŋ)   kite-flying (ˈkaɪtˌflaɪɪŋ)
wonderful (ˈwʌndɚfəl)   babysitter (ˈbebɪˌsɪtɚ)
companion (kəmˈpænjən)   full (fʊl)
wisdom (ˈwɪzdəm)   explain (ɪkˈsplen)
wrong (rɔŋ)   teach (titʃ)
honest (ˈɑnɪst)   fair (fɛr)

Gram and gramps are family leaders.
They carry on old traditions.
They pass on stories of our ancestors.

My grandparents hold my family
   together.
They keep everyone in harmony.
Every family member cherishes and
   respects them.

I never take them for granted.
I know they won't live forever.
But they'll always be a part of my life.

4

---

gram〔græm〕
leader〔'lidə〕
tradition〔trə'dɪʃən〕
ancestor〔'ænsɛstə〕
keep〔kip〕
in harmony
cherish〔'tʃɛrɪʃ〕
take…for granted
always〔'ɔlwez〕

gramps〔græmps〕
carry on
pass on
hold together
harmony〔'harmənɪ〕
member〔'mɛmbə〕
respect〔rɪ'spɛkt〕
forever〔fə'ɛvə〕
part〔part〕

4. My Grandparents

○ 演講解說

My grandparents are so sweet.	我的祖父母非常和藹。
They hold a special place in my heart.	他們在我心目中的地位很特別。
They're more precious than gold.	他們比黃金還要珍貴。
They worked hard all their lives.	他們辛勤工作一輩子。
They sacrificed for my family.	他們爲了我的家人犧牲奉獻。
They raised my parents very well.	他們把我的父母教養得非常好。
I owe them thanks and praise.	我應該感謝並讚美他們。
I'm alive because of them.	因爲他們，我才能活在這個世界上。
I don't know how to repay them.	我不知道該如何報答他們。

** ————————————

grandparents〔'græn͵pɛrənts〕n. pl. 祖父母

sweet〔swit〕adj. 和藹的；溫柔的　　hold〔hold〕v. 擁有；佔據

special〔'spɛʃəl〕adj. 特別的　　place〔ples〕n. 地位　　heart〔hɑrt〕n. 心

precious〔'prɛʃəs〕adj. 珍貴的　　gold〔gold〕n. 黃金

hard〔hɑrd〕adv. 努力地　　*all one's life* 一輩子；終生

sacrifice〔'sækrə͵faɪs〕v. 犧牲　　raise〔rez〕v. 教養；撫養

parents〔'pɛrənts〕n. pl. 父母　　owe〔o〕v. 欠；應給予

thank〔θæŋk〕n. 感謝　　praise〔prez〕n. 讚美

alive〔ə'laɪv〕adj. 活著的　　repay〔rɪ'pe〕v. 報答

My grandparents are special friends. | 我的祖父母是很特別的朋友。
They're easygoing and understanding. | 他們既隨和又明事理。
They're easier to talk to than my parents. | 他們比我的父母還好商量。

My grandma makes me delicious foods. | 我祖母會煮好吃的東西給我吃。
My grandpa takes me fishing and kite-flying. | 我祖父會帶我去釣魚和放風箏。
They are wonderful babysitters and companions. | 他們是很棒的褓母和夥伴。

They are full of wisdom, too. | 他們還充滿了智慧。
They explain right and wrong. | 他們能夠說明是非。
They teach me to be honest and fair. | 他們教我要誠實且公正。

4

** ———————————

easygoing〔'izɪ'goɪŋ〕adj. 隨遇而安的；隨和的
understanding〔͵ʌndɚ'stændɪŋ〕adj. 明白事理的
talk〔tɔk〕v. 說話；商量　　grandma〔'grænma〕n. 祖母
make〔mek〕v. 準備；烹調　　delicious〔dɪ'lɪʃəs〕adj. 美味的
grandpa〔'grænpa〕n. 祖父　　take〔tek〕v. 帶（某人）去
fishing〔'fɪʃɪŋ〕n. 釣魚　　kite-flying〔'kaɪt͵flaɪɪŋ〕n. 放風箏
babysitter〔'bebɪ͵sɪtɚ〕n.（臨時）褓母
companion〔kəm'pænjən〕n. 夥伴　　wisdom〔'wɪzdəm〕n. 智慧
explain〔ɪk'splen〕v. 說明　　*right and wrong* 對與錯；是與非
honest〔'ɑnɪst〕adj. 誠實的　　fair〔fɛr〕adj. 公平的

***Gram and gramps are family leaders*.**

祖父母是一家之主。

They carry on old traditions.

他們延續古老的傳統。

They pass on stories of our ancestors.

他們把祖先的故事流傳下來。

My grandparents hold my family together.

祖父母使我們家族團結一致。

They keep everyone in harmony.

他們讓每個人和睦相處。

Every family member cherishes and respects them.

每位家庭成員都很珍視且尊敬他們。

I never take them for granted.

我絕不會忽視他們。

I know they won't live forever.

我知道他們不會永遠活著。

But they'll always be a part of my life.

但是他們在我的生命中，永遠都是很重要的一部份。

** ————————————————

gram〔græm〕*n.* 祖母　gramps〔græmps〕*n.* 祖父
leader〔'lidɚ〕*n.* 領導者　*carry on* 繼續
tradition〔trə'dɪʃən〕*n.* 傳統　*pass on* 傳遞
ancestor〔'ænsɛstɚ〕*n.* 祖先　*hold together* 使團結
keep〔kip〕*v.* 使維持　harmony〔'harmənɪ〕*n.* 和睦；融洽
in harmony 和睦融洽　member〔'mɛmbɚ〕*n.* 成員
cherish〔'tʃɛrɪʃ〕*v.* 珍視；珍惜　respect〔rɪ'spɛkt〕*v.* 尊敬
take…for granted 視…爲理所當然；（因視爲當然而）不予重視
forever〔fɚ'ɛvɚ〕*adv.* 永遠地　part〔part〕*n.* 部份；重要部分

背景說明

　　俗話說:「家有一老,如有一寶。」你曾經跟祖父母住在一起過嗎?他們是很嚴厲,還是很和藹可親呢?本篇演講稿,要教你用英文來介紹祖父母,把你對他們的印象告訴大家。

1. *My grandparents are so sweet.*
   grandparents〔'græn,pɛrənts〕 *n. pl.* 祖父母
   so〔so〕 *adv.* 非常
   sweet〔swit〕 *adj.* 和藹的;溫柔的

　　sweet 的基本意思是「甜的」,但在這裡是作「和藹的;溫柔的」解 (= *kind*)。所以,這句話的意思是「我的祖父母非常和藹。」也可說成:

My gram and gramps are so kind.
(我祖母和祖父都非常和藹。)

My grandparents are so lovable!
(我的祖父母都非常可愛!)

gram〔græm〕 *n.* 祖母
gramps〔græmps〕 *n.* 祖父
kind〔kaɪnd〕 *adj.* 親切的;和藹的
lovable〔'lʌvəbḷ〕 *adj.* 可愛的

4

2. ***They hold a special place in my heart.***

hold〔hold〕*v.* 擁有；佔據
special〔'spɛʃəl〕*adj.* 特別的
place〔ples〕*n.* 地位　　heart〔hɑrt〕*n.* 心

　　　hold 的基本意思是「抓住；拿著」，但在此引申爲「擁有；佔據」(= *have ; occupy*)，而 place 則是作「位置；地位」解，所以整句話的意思是「他們在我心目中的地位很特別。」以下都是美國人常說的話，我們依照使用頻率排列：

① They mean so much to me.【第一常用】
　　（他們對我來說意義重大。）

② They mean a lot to me.【第二常用】
　　（他們對我來說意義重大。）

③ I love them very much.【第三常用】
　　（我很愛他們。）

④ ***They hold a special place in my heart.***

⑤ They are near and dear to me.
　　（他們對我來說，是很親的人。）

⑥ I care about them very much.
　　（我很在乎他們。）

⑦ I consider them very special people.
　　（我認爲他們是很特別的人。）

mean〔min〕*v.* 有…的意義　　love〔lʌv〕*v.* 愛
near and dear 親近的　　***care about*** 在乎；關心
consider〔kən'sɪdɚ〕*v.* 認爲

3. **They're more precious than gold.**

precious〔'prɛʃəs〕*adj.* 珍貴的　　gold〔gold〕*n.* 黃金

這句話的意思是「他們比黃金還要珍貴。」主要是要強調祖父母的重要性，所以 gold 也可以用其他貴重的東西來代替，像是 diamond（鑽石）。這句話也可説成：

They're more important than anything.
（他們比任何東西都重要。）

They are priceless to me.
（他們對我來說是無價的。）

important〔ɪm'pɔrtn̩t〕*adj.* 重要的
priceless〔'praɪslɪs〕*adj.* 無價的；非常貴重的

4

4. **They raised my parents very well.**

raise〔rez〕*v.* 教養；撫養　　parents〔'pɛrənts〕*n. pl.* 父母

raise 的主要意思是「舉起」，在此引申為「教養；撫養」(= *bring up*)，所以這句話的意思是「他們把我的父母教養得很好。」也可以説成：

They were great parents to my parents.
（對我的父母來說，他們是很棒的父母。）

They brought up my parents in an excellent way.
（他們以很優秀的方式來教養我的父母。）

great〔gret〕*adj.* 很棒的　　***bring up*** 教養；撫養長大
excellent〔'ɛkslənt〕*adj.* 極好的　　way〔we〕*n.* 方式

5. ***My grandma makes me delicious foods.***

grandma〔'grænmɑ〕*n.* 祖母

make〔mek〕*v.* 準備;烹調

delicious〔dɪ'lɪʃəs〕*adj.* 美味的　　food〔fud〕*n.* 食物

　　　make 原本的意思是「做」,在此引申爲「準備;烹調」(*=prepare ; cook*),所以這句話的意思是「我祖母會煮好吃的東西給我吃。」也可以説成:

My grandma cooks tasty foods.

(我祖母會煮好吃的東西。)

My grandmother prepares yummy things for
　me to eat. (我祖母會準備好吃的食物給我吃。)

cook〔kʊk〕*v.* 烹調;煮　　tasty〔'testɪ〕*adj.* 好吃的

prepare〔prɪ'pɛr〕*v.* 準備　　yummy〔'jʌmɪ〕*adj.* 好吃的

6. ***They explain right and wrong.***

explain〔ɪk'splen〕*v.* 解釋;說明

right and wrong 對與錯;是與非

　　　這句話是由 They explain what is right and wrong. 省略而來的,意思是「他們能夠說明是非。」也可説成:

They teach me how to do it. (他們敎我該怎麼做。)

My grandparents help me distinguish what is
　good and what is bad.

(我的祖父母幫我分辨是非。)

【teach〔titʃ〕*v.* 敎　　distinguish〔dɪ'stɪŋgwɪʃ〕*v.* 分辨】

7. *They carry on old traditions*.
   carry on 繼續　　tradition〔trəˋdɪʃən〕*n.* 傳統

   　　　　carry on 是作「繼續」（= *continue*）解，所以這
   句話的意思是「他們延續古老的傳統。」也可說成：
   They maintain our family customs.（他們延續我們
   的家族習俗。）【maintain〔menˋten〕*v.* 繼續；維持
   custom〔ˋkʌstəm〕*n.* 習俗】

8. *My grandparents hold my family together*.
   hold together 使團結

4

   　　　　這句話的意思是「祖父母使我們家族團結一致。」
   祖父母的存在，可以調節父母親那一輩的糾紛，讓整
   個家族和樂融融，非常重要。

   這句話也可說成：

   　　My gram and gramps keep my family united.
   　　（我祖母和祖父使我們家族團結一致。）
   　　They keep us from falling apart.
   　　（他們使我們免於分裂。）

   　　keep〔kip〕*v.* 使維持（某種狀態）
   　　united〔juˋnaɪtɪd〕*adj.* 團結的
   　　keep…from 使…免於
   　　fall apart 分裂

9. ***I never take them for granted.***

take…for granted 視…為理所當然；（因視為當然而）不予重視

　　這句話的字面意思是「我絕不會視他們為理所當然。」引申為「我絕不會忽視他們。」也可以說成：I never ignore them.（我絕不會忽視他們。）
【ignore〔ɪgˋnor〕*v.* 忽視】

　　另外，***take…for granted*** 是作「視…為理所當然；（因視為當然而）不予重視」解，例如：

Never ***take*** good health ***for granted.***
（不要把健康視為理所當然。）

Time flies by — don't ***take*** it ***for granted.***
（光陰飛逝 —— 不要把時間視為理當然。）

He ***takes for granted*** all that I do for him.
（他把我為他所做的一切視為理所當然。）

Sadly, we ***take*** many wonderful things
　for granted.
（遺憾的是，我們把許多美好的事物視為理所當然。）

health〔hɛlθ〕*n.* 健康
fly〔flaɪ〕*v.*（時間）飛也似地過去
fly by 時間（飛逝）　　sadly〔ˋsædlɪ〕*adv.* 遺憾的是
wonderful〔ˋwʌndɚfəl〕*adj.* 很棒的；美好的

○作文範例

My Grandparents

My grandparents are very special to me. They have worked hard all their lives and sacrificed a lot for my family. Not only that, but they are also special friends to me. They are easier to talk to than my parents and they are very kind to me. *For example*, my grandmother makes me delicious things to eat and my grandfather often takes me fishing.

In addition, they are the leaders of my family. They are full of wisdom and know the stories of our ancestors. They are the ones that hold our family together. *As a result*, I owe them a great deal, but I don't know how to repay them. All I can do is cherish them and never take them for granted.

● 中文翻譯

我的祖父母

　　對我來說，我的祖父母很特別。他們辛勤工作一輩子，並為我的家庭做了很大的犧牲。不只是那樣，他們對我來說，也是很特別的朋友。他們比我的父母還好商量，而且他們對我很親切。例如，我祖母會煮好吃的東西給我吃，然後我祖父常常帶我去釣魚。

　　另外，他們是一家之主。他們充滿智慧，而且還知道祖先的故事。他們使我們的家族團結一致。所以，我欠他們很多，但是我不知道該怎麼回報他們。我所能做的，就是珍惜他們，並且絕不忽視他們。

5. My Favorite Pet

My favorite pets are dogs.
I smile when I see one.
I play with them when I can.

Dogs aren't animals to me.
They're perfect companions.
They're man's best friends.

Dogs are loyal and honest.
Their eyes are like windows.
I can see right into their hearts.

5

favorite (ˈfevərɪt)
smile (smaɪl)
perfect (ˈpɝfɪkt)
companion (kəmˈpænjən)
loyal (ˈlɔɪəl)
eye (aɪ)
window (ˈwɪndo)
right (raɪt)

pet (pɛt)
animal (ˈænəml̩)

man (mæn)
honest (ˈɑnɪst)
like (laɪk)
see into
heart (hɑrt)

5

Dogs are unique.

No two are alike.

Each one has its own personality.

The little ones are cute.

The big ones are frisky.

Their wagging tails are funny.

I love shaggy dogs.

I love playful dogs.

I wouldn't mind being a dog.

unique〔 ju'nik 〕

own〔 on 〕

cute〔 kjut 〕

wagging〔'wægɪŋ 〕

funny〔'fʌnɪ 〕

playful〔'plefəl 〕

be〔 bɪ 〕

alike〔 ə'laɪk 〕

personality〔ˌpɝsn̩'ælətɪ 〕

frisky〔'frɪskɪ 〕

tail〔 tel 〕

shaggy〔'ʃægɪ 〕

mind〔 maɪnd 〕

***Dogs are bright*.**

They can do tricks.

They can be useful, too.

Guide dogs lead the blind.

Rescue dogs save people.

Search dogs help the police.

5

Dogs know how to live.

They're happy-go-lucky.

I hope I can have one someday.

bright (braɪt)

useful ('jusfəl)

lead (lid)

the blind

save (sev)

police (pə'lis)

happy-go-lucky ('hæpɪˌgo'lʌkɪ)

hope (hop)

trick (trɪk)

guide dog

blind (blaɪnd)

rescue ('rɛskju)

search (sɝtʃ)

live (lɪv)

someday ('sʌmˌde)

5. My Favorite Pet

○ 演講解說

My favorite pets are dogs.	我最喜歡的寵物是狗。
I smile when I see one.	我看到狗的時候會微笑。
I play with them when I can.	我有空就會跟牠們玩。
Dogs aren't animals to me.	狗對我來說不算是動物。
They're perfect companions.	牠們是理想的夥伴。
They're man's best friends.	牠們是人類最好的朋友。
Dogs are loyal and honest.	狗既忠心又誠實。
Their eyes are like windows.	牠們的眼睛就像窗戶一樣。
I can see right into their hearts.	我可以直接看透牠們的心。

** ─────────────────

favorite〔'fevərɪt〕adj. 最喜歡的　　pet〔pɛt〕n. 寵物
smile〔smaɪl〕v. 微笑　　animal〔'ænəml〕n. 動物
perfect〔'pɝfɪkt〕adj. 完美的；理想的
companion〔kəm'pænjən〕n. 同伴；夥伴　　man〔mæn〕n. 人
loyal〔'lɔɪəl〕adj. 忠心的　　honest〔'ɑnɪst〕adj. 誠實的
eye〔aɪ〕n. 眼睛　　like〔laɪk〕prep. 像
window〔'wɪndo〕n. 窗戶　　*see into* 看透
right〔raɪt〕adv. 直接地　　heart〔hɑrt〕n. 心

Dogs are unique.

No two are alike.

Each one has its own
   personality.

The little ones are cute.

The big ones are frisky.

Their wagging tails are funny.

I love shaggy dogs.

I love playful dogs.

I wouldn't mind being a dog.

狗是與衆不同的。

沒有兩隻狗是一樣的。

每隻狗都有自己的個性。

小狗很可愛。

大狗很活潑。

牠們搖擺的尾巴很有趣。

我喜歡毛茸茸的狗。

我喜歡頑皮的狗。

我不介意當一隻狗。

5

** ──────────────

unique〔ju'nik〕*adj.* 獨一無二的；與衆不同的

alike〔ə'laɪk〕*adj.* 同樣的；相像的　　own〔on〕*adj.* 自己的

personality〔͵pɝsn̩'ælətɪ〕*n.* 個性

cute〔kjut〕*adj.* 可愛的　　frisky〔'frɪskɪ〕*adj.* 活潑的

wagging〔'wægɪŋ〕*adj.* 搖擺的　　tail〔tel〕*n.* 尾巴

funny〔'fʌnɪ〕*adj.* 有趣的　　shaggy〔'ʃægɪ〕*adj.* 毛茸茸的

playful〔'plefəl〕*adj.* 頑皮的　　mind〔maɪnd〕*v.* 介意

be〔bɪ〕*v.* 成爲

Dogs are bright.	狗很聰明。
They can do tricks.	牠們會表演特技。
They can be useful, too.	牠們也很能幹。
Guide dogs lead the blind.	導盲犬會引導盲人。
Rescue dogs save people.	救援犬會救人。
Search dogs help the police.	搜索犬會幫警察的忙。
Dogs know how to live.	狗知道怎麼生存。
They're happy-go-lucky.	牠們無憂無慮。
I hope I can have one someday.	我希望有一天我也能有一隻狗。

5

＊＊ ——————————————————

bright〔braɪt〕*adj.* 聰明的　　trick〔trɪk〕*n.* 特技；把戲
useful〔'jusfəl〕*adj.* 有用的；能幹的　　***guide dog*** 導盲犬
lead〔lid〕*v.* 帶領；引導　　blind〔blaɪnd〕*adj.* 失明的
the blind 盲人　　rescue〔'rɛskjʊ〕*adj.* 救難的
save〔sev〕*v.* 拯救　　search〔sɝtʃ〕*n.* 搜索
police〔pə'lis〕*n.* 警察　　live〔lɪv〕*v.* 生存
happy-go-lucky〔'hæpɪˌgo'lʌkɪ〕*adj.* 隨遇而安的；無憂無慮的
hope〔hop〕*v.* 希望
someday〔'sʌmˌde〕*adv.* （將來）有一天

● 背景說明

　　養寵物其實是一種很好的休閒活動，科學研究顯示，養寵物有益健康，寵物雖然不會說話，但是牠們會耐心地陪伴在你身邊，分享你的快樂與悲傷。本篇演講稿，要教你如何向別人介紹自己最喜歡的寵物。

1. *I play with them when I can.*

　　這句話的字面意思是「當我可以的時候，就會和牠們玩。」引申為「我有空就會跟牠們玩。」這句話源自 I play with them when I can spare the time. （當我可以空出時間時，就會和他們玩。）或 I like to play with them whenever I can.

（每當我有空，就喜歡和牠們玩。）

【spare〔spɛr〕*v.* 騰出（時間）
whenever〔hwɛn'ɛvɚ〕*conj.* 每當】

這句話也可說成：

When I'm free, I enjoy playing with dogs.
（我有空的時候，喜歡跟狗玩。）

Whenever I have a chance, I enjoy playing
　　with dogs. （我一有機會，就喜歡跟狗玩。）

free〔fri〕*adj.* 有空閒的　　chance〔tʃæns〕*n.* 機會
enjoy〔ɪn'dʒɔɪ〕*v.* 喜歡

2. ***Dogs aren't animals to me.***
animal〔'ænəml̩〕 *n.* 動物

　　這句話的意思是「狗對我來說不算是動物。」很
多人都認同「狗是人類最忠實的朋友。」在他們眼
裡，狗和一般的動物是不同的。這句話也可說成：

I don't consider dogs to be just animals.
（我不認爲狗只是動物。）

I don't regard dogs as mere animals.
（我不認爲狗只是動物。）

consider〔kən'sɪdɚ〕 *v.* 認爲
regard〔rɪ'gɑrd〕 *v.* 認爲　　mere〔mɪr〕 *adj.* 僅僅；只

　　另外，在本句中，"***to sb.***" 是作「對某人來說」
解，以下都是美國人喜歡說的話：

It doesn't matter ***to me***.（對我而言，那不重要。）

To me, time is money.
（對我來說，時間就是金錢。）

To my family, honesty is the best policy.
（對我家來說，誠實爲上策。）

To my mother, anyone who lies is dishonest.
（對我媽來說，說謊的人就是不誠實。）

matter〔'mætɚ〕 *v.* 關係重要
honesty〔'ɑnɪstɪ〕 *n.* 誠實　　policy〔'pɑləsɪ〕 *n.* 政策
lie〔laɪ〕 *v.* 說謊　　dishonest〔dɪs'ɑnɪst〕 *adj.* 不誠實的

3. *Their eyes are like windows.*

eye〔aɪ〕*n.* 眼睛　　like〔laɪk〕*prep.* 像
window〔'wɪndo〕*n.* 窗戶

　　like 的基本意思是「喜歡」，但在這裡，是當介系詞用，作「像」解，所以這句話的意思是「牠們的眼睛就像窗戶一樣。」也可說成：

A dog's eyes reveal what he's feeling.
（小狗的眼睛會透露出牠的感受。）

It's easy to read a dog's mind through
　　his eyes.
（要從小狗的眼睛看出牠的心思很容易。）

reveal〔rɪ'vil〕*v.* 顯示；透露
feel〔fil〕*v.* 感覺　　easy〔'izɪ〕*adj.* 容易的
read** one's **mind 看出某人的心思
through〔θru〕*prep.* 透過

　　另外，like 常作「像」解，例如：

He acts *like* an adult. (他的行為像大人一樣。)

His loud voice is *like* thunder.
（他的大嗓門像雷一樣。）

My dad's new truck is *like* a tank.
（我爸的新卡車像坦克一樣）

act〔ækt〕*v.* 行為；舉止　　adult〔ə'dʌlt〕*n.* 大人；成人
loud〔laʊd〕*adj.* 大的；宏亮的
voice〔vɔɪs〕*n.* 嗓子；聲音　　thunder〔'θʌndɚ〕*n.* 雷
truck〔trʌk〕*n.* 卡車　　tank〔tæŋk〕*n.* 坦克車

5

4. *I can see right into their hearts.*

   see into 看透 　 right〔raɪt〕*adv.* 直接地

   heart〔hɑrt〕*n.* 心

   　　　　這句話的意思是「我可以直接看透牠們的心。」也

   可說成：It's easy to understand their feelings.（要

   了解牠們的感受很容易。）【understand〔͵ʌndə'stænd〕*v.*

   了解　 feeling〔'filɪŋ〕*n.* 感受】

   see into 是作「看透」(= *understand*) 解，例如：

   > My parents know me so well that they can
   > 　　always *see* right *into* me.
   >
   > （我的父母很了解我，他們總是能直接看透我的心思。）
   >
   > Fortune-tellers claim they can *see into* the
   > 　　future.（算命師宣稱他們可以看透未來。）

   parents〔'pɛrənts〕*n. pl.* 父母

   fortune-teller〔'fɔrtʃən͵tɛlə〕*n.* 算命師

   claim〔klem〕*v.* 宣稱　 future〔'fjutʃə〕*n.* 未來

5. *No two are alike.*

   alike〔ə'laɪk〕*adj.* 同樣的；相像的

   　　　　這句話的意思是「沒有兩隻狗是一樣的。」源自

   No two dogs are exactly alike.（沒有兩隻狗是完

   全相同的。）也可說成：None are the same.（沒有

   一模一樣的狗。）【exactly〔ɪg'zæktlɪ〕*adv.* 完全地

   none〔nʌn〕*pron.* 一個也沒有　 same〔sem〕*adj.* 相同的】

6. *I wouldn't mind being a dog.*

mind〔maɪnd〕*v.* 介意

這句話的意思是「我不介意
當一隻狗。」也可說成：

For me, being a dog would be OK.
（對我來說，當狗也不錯。）

I don't think being a dog would be bad.
（我不覺得當狗有什麼不好。）

【OK〔'o'ke〕*adj.* 不錯的】

mind 的基本意思是「心；想法」，在此當動詞
用，作「介意；反對」(= *care about* ; *object to*)
解，例如：

Do you *mind* if I go first?
（你介意我先嗎？）

Do you *mind* if I borrow your pen?
（你介意把筆借給我嗎？）

I wouldn't *mind* eating fast food every day.
（我不介意每天吃速食。）
【要特別注意的是，mind 後面若要接動詞，只能接
動名詞 (V-ing)，不能接不定詞 (to V.)】

first〔fɝst〕*adv.* 先
borrow〔'bɑro〕*v.* 借（入）　　*fast food* 速食

5

7. *They can do tricks.*

trick〔trɪk〕*n.* 特技；把戲　　***do trick*** 表演特技

    trick 指的是 a special skill（特別的技巧），所以這句話的意思是「牠們會表演特技。」經過訓練的狗，會表演很多特技，常見的有：catch a ball（接球）、sit up（坐好）、shake hands（握手）、play dead（裝死）等，非常有趣。

    trick 作「特技；把戲」解，例如：

> You can't teach an old dog new *tricks*.
> (【諺】老狗學不會新把戲。)
> Clowns perform *tricks* at the circus.
> (小丑在馬戲團裡表演特技。)
> Juggling is a very popular *trick*.
> (變魔術是很受歡迎的特技表演。)

teach〔titʃ〕*v.* 教　　clown〔klaʊn〕*n.* 小丑
perform〔pə'fɔrm〕*v.* 表演
circus〔'sɝkəs〕*n.* 馬戲團
juggling〔'dʒʌglɪŋ〕*n.* 變戲法；變魔術
popular〔'pɑpjələ〕*adj.* 受歡迎的

    要注意的是，要說「表演特技」可以用 do a trick 或 perform a trick，但是不能說成 play a trick，因為此時 trick 的意思是「捉弄；開玩笑」。

【比較】*They can do tricks.*【正】
       They can perform tricks.【正】
       (牠們會表演特技。)
       They can play tricks.【誤】

○作文範例

My Favorite Pet

My favorite pets are dogs. *In my opinion*, dogs are the perfect companions. *For one thing*, they are loyal. My dog is always happy to see me. *For another*, they are unique. No two dogs are exactly alike, either in appearance or personality. *In addition*, dogs are bright. They can do tricks and even work to help people. *For example*, dogs can learn to lead the blind or help the police. *Finally*, dogs really know how to live. They never worry about the future or suffer from bad moods. *In fact*, dogs are so wonderful that I wouldn't mind being one.

5

● 中文翻譯

我最喜歡的寵物

狗是我最喜歡的寵物。依我之見,狗是最完美的夥伴。首先,牠們很忠誠。我的狗總是很高興見到我。再來,牠們是獨一無二的。沒有兩隻狗是一模一樣的,不管是外表或個性。另外,狗很聰明。牠們會表演特技,而且甚至會努力幫助人們。例如,狗可以學會引導盲人,或是幫警察的忙。最後,狗很了解要如何生活。牠們從不擔心未來,或是心情不好。事實上,狗非常棒,所以我不介意當一隻狗。

6. My Neighborhood

My neighborhood is nice.
It's my home sweet home.
I feel comfortable there.

I live in the city.
My home is in a high rise.
It's quiet, safe and clean.

The location is convenient.
Everything we need is nearby.
I can walk to school in minutes.

6

neighborhood ('nebə͵hʊd)
sweet (swit)   comfortable ('kʌmfə-təbḷ)
live (lɪv)   city ('sɪtɪ)
high rise ('haɪ'raɪz) quiet ('kwaɪət)
safe (sef)   clean (klin)
location (lo'keʃən)   convenient (kən'vinjənt)
nearby ('nɪr'baɪ)   in (ɪn)
minute ('mɪnɪt)

My neighbors are friendly.

Everyone is kind and polite.

Everyone smiles and says hello.

We watch out for each other.

We care about the environment.

We always hold cleanup activities.

I like the older neighbors best.

They are gentle and sweet.

They often give me food and
  other treats.

6

neighbor ('nebɚ)   friendly ('frɛndlɪ)
kind (kaɪnd)   polite (pə'laɪt)
smile (smaɪl)   hello (hə'lo)
watch out for   *each other*
care about   environment (ɪn'vaɪrənmənt)
always ('ɔlwez)   hold (hold)
cleanup ('klin,ʌp)   activity (æk'tɪvətɪ)
best (bɛst)   gentle ('dʒɛntl̩)
treat (trit)

There is a small park close by.

It has a new playground.

That's where I play with friends.

My community is special.

It's perfect to me.

I'd never want to move.

How's your neighborhood?

Do you like where you live?

I hope you love your home, too.

6

---

small (smɔl)   park (pɑrk)

close by   playground ('ple͵graʊnd)

community (kə'mjunətɪ)

special ('spɛʃəl)   perfect ('pɝfɪkt)

want (wɑnt)   move (muv)

hope (hop)   love (lʌv)

6. My Neighborhood

演講解說

My neighborhood is nice.　　我家附近很不錯。
It's my home sweet home.　　那是我的家，甜蜜的家。
I feel comfortable there.　　我在那裡覺得很自在。

I live in the city.　　我住在城市裡。
My home is in a high rise.　　我家在一棟大廈裡。
It's quiet, safe and clean.　　我家寧靜、安全而且乾淨。

The location is convenient.　　那個地點很方便。
Everything we need is nearby.　　我們需要的一切都在附近。
I can walk to school in　　我可以在幾分鐘之內走到
　minutes.　　學校。

**　

neighborhood〔'nebə͵hud〕*n.* 鄰近地區
sweet〔swit〕*adj.* 甜蜜的；親切的
comfortable〔'kʌmfətəbḷ〕*adj.* 舒服自在的　　live〔lɪv〕*v.* 住
city〔'sɪtɪ〕*n.* 城市　　high rise〔'haɪ͵raɪz〕*n.* 高層建築；大廈
quiet〔'kwaɪət〕*adj.* 安靜的　　safe〔sef〕*adj.* 安全的
clean〔klin〕*adj.* 乾淨的　　location〔lo'keʃən〕*n.* 位置；地點
convenient〔kən'vinjənt〕*adj.* 方便的　　nearby〔'nɪr'baɪ〕*adv.* 在附近
in〔ɪn〕*prep.* 在…（時間）內　　minute〔'mɪnɪt〕*n.* 分鐘

My neighbors are friendly.	我的鄰居都很友善。
Everyone is kind and polite.	每個人都親切又有禮貌。
Everyone smiles and says hello.	每個人都會微笑著打招呼。
We watch out for each other.	我們會替彼此留意。
We care about the environment.	我們關心環境。
We always hold cleanup activities.	我們總是會舉行清潔活動。
I like the older neighbors best.	我最喜歡年長的鄰居。
They are gentle and sweet.	他們和藹又親切。
They often give me food and other treats.	他們常給我食物，還有其他甜點。

6

＊＊

neighbor〔'nebɚ〕*n.* 鄰居　　friendly〔'frɛndlɪ〕*adj.* 友善的
kind〔kaɪnd〕*adj.* 親切的　　polite〔pə'laɪt〕*adj.* 有禮貌的
smile〔smaɪl〕*v.* 微笑
hello〔hə'lo〕*n.* hello 的問候聲；打招呼
say hello 問好；打招呼　　*watch out for* 留意；注意
each other 彼此　　*care about* 關心
environment〔ɪn'vaɪrəmənt〕*n.* 環境　　hold〔hold〕*v.* 舉行
cleanup〔'klinˌʌp〕*n.* 清潔　　activity〔æk'tɪvətɪ〕*n.* 活動
best〔bɛst〕*adv.* 最…　　gentle〔'dʒɛntḷ〕*adj.* 和藹的
treat〔trit〕*n.* 很棒的東西；美食；甜點

There is a small park close by.	附近有座小公園。
It has a new playground.	裡面有個新的遊樂場。
That's where I play with friends.	那就是我和朋友一起玩的地方。
My community is special.	我的社區很特別。
It's perfect to me.	它對我來說很完美。
I'd never want to move.	我永遠都不要搬走。
How's your neighborhood?	你家附近如何？
Do you like where you live?	你喜歡你住的地方嗎？
I hope you love your home, too.	我希望你也愛你的家。

6

＊＊ ─────────────────

small〔smɔl〕*adj.* 小的

park〔pɑrk〕*n.* 公園　　***close by*** 在附近

playground〔'ple͵graʊnd〕*n.* 遊樂場；運動場

community〔kə'mjunətɪ〕*n.* 社區

special〔'spɛʃəl〕*adj.* 特別的

perfect〔'pɝfɪkt〕*adj.* 完美的　　move〔muv〕*v.* 搬家

hope〔hop〕*v.* 希望　　love〔lʌv〕*v.* 愛

◉ 背景說明

　　從小，老師就教我們要「敦親睦鄰」、「守望相助」，要和鄰居好好相處。在平時，鄰居或許看起來不像親戚那麼重要，但是當緊急事件發生時，住在附近的人，卻是能夠馬上伸出援手來幫你的朋友。

1. ***It's my home sweet home.***
   sweet〔swit〕*adj.* 甜蜜的

　　　　home sweet home 是源自美國作家兼演員 John Howard Payne 所作的歌詞 "home, home, sweet, sweet home"（家！家！甜蜜，甜蜜的家）。美國人非常喜歡這句話，他們每天回到家都講，而且甚至會把這句話貼在家裡的任何地方，非常有趣。

　　　　這句話的字面意思是「那是我的家，甜蜜的家。」重複說兩次 home，是要強調家有多棒，所以整句話引申的意思是「我家是全世界最棒的地方。」(= *My house is a wonderful place.*)

　　　　同樣的意思，美國人還有很多種說法，我們依照使用頻率排列如下：

　　① ***It's my home sweet home.***【第一常用】

　　② **There's no place like home.**【第二常用】
　　　　（沒有一個地方像家一樣。）

6

③ My home is the best. 【第三常用】
（我家是最棒的。）

④ North, south, east, or west, home is the best.
（東奔西跑，不如家裡最好；家是最棒的地方。）

⑤ I love my home more than any place.
（我愛我的家勝過任何地方。）

⑥ My home is the perfect place to me.
（我家對我來說是完美無缺的。）

north〔nɔrθ〕n. 北方　　south〔savθ〕n. 南方
east〔ist〕n. 東方　　west〔wɛst〕n. 西方
more than 超過　　perfect〔ˈpɜfɪkt〕adj. 完美的

6

2. ***My home is in a high rise.***
high rise〔ˈhaɪˈraɪz〕n. 高層建築；大廈

　　high rise 是指有很多層的建築物，而且裡面通常附有電梯。整句話的意思是「我家在一棟大廈裡。」也可以說成：I live in a tall building.（我住在一棟高樓裡。）

　　台灣的住宅，大約可分為下列四種，當你要介紹自己住的地方時，可以把 high rise 代換成下列其中一種：

① cottage〔ˈkɑtɪdʒ〕n. 單棟
住宅或別墅（= *house*）
【也就是所謂的透天厝；台灣
中南部有很多這樣的住宅。】

cottage

② town house (市內住宅)

　　【這是台灣最常見的住宅類型。】

③ high rise (公寓大樓)

　　【這是比較現代化的建築物，通常會蓋到十幾、二十層樓。】

④ condominium〔ˌkɑndə'mɪnɪəm〕n. 戶主共管的公寓
　　(= condo)

　　【這類住宅在台灣有愈來愈多的趨勢，整棟建築物本身，就
　　　像一個小型社區，有花園或游泳池等公共設施，而且通常
　　　會由居民共同組成管理委員會。】

town house

high rise

condominium

6

3. *I can walk to school in minutes.*

　in〔ɪn〕prep. 在…（時間）內
　minute〔'mɪnɪt〕n. 分鐘

　　　　這句話的意思是「我可以在幾分鐘之內走到學校。」
　in 這個介系詞是作「在…（時間）內」(= within) 解，
　例如：You can fly from N.Y. to L.A. *in* hours. (你
　可以在幾小時內，從紐約飛到洛杉磯。)

　fly〔flaɪ〕v. 飛；搭飛機　　*N.Y.* 紐約 (= *New York*)
　L.A. 洛杉磯 (= *Los Angeles*)

4. **We watch out for each other.**

watch out for 留意；注意　　**each other** 彼此；互相

這句話的意思是「我們會替彼此留意。」也就是
中國人所說的「守望相助」。整句話還可以說成：

We look out for one another.
（我們會替彼此留意。）
We all help each other out.
（我們都會互相幫忙。）
【**look out for** 留心；注意　　**help** sb. **out** 幫助某人】

另外，如果只有 watch out 這兩個字，則是用在
提醒別人注意突發狀況，意思是「小心！」例如：**Watch
out!** There is a car coming.（小心！有車來了。）

6

5. **I like the older neighbors best.**

best〔bɛst〕adv. 最⋯

這句話的意思是「我最喜歡
年長的鄰居。」它是由 I like the
older neighbors *the* best. 省略而來，
best 當副詞時，美國人口語上常常會省略 the，例如：

Next Friday would suit me **best.**
（下星期五對我來說最合適。）
Which book do you like **best?**
（你最喜歡哪一本書？）
【suit〔sut〕v. 適合】

6. ***They often give me food and other treats***.

treat〔trit〕*n.* 很棒的東西；美食；甜點

　　　treat 當名詞用，基本意思是「請客」，例如，
This is my treat.（這次我請客。）但在這句話裡，
treat 是作「很棒的東西；美食；甜點」解，通常是
指糖果餅乾之類的。所以整句話的意思是「他們常
給我食物，還有其他甜點。」

treat 作「甜點」解，舉例如下：

　　　I've got a ***treat*** for you after supper.
　　　（晚飯後，我要給你一份甜點。）

　　　A big ice-cream cone on a hot day is
　　　　a real ***treat***.
　　　（在大熱天裡，蛋捲冰淇淋真的是很棒的點心。）

　　　supper〔'sʌpɚ〕*n.* 晚餐
　　　ice-cream cone 蛋捲冰淇淋　　real〔'riəl〕*adj.* 真的

6

另外，這句話還可以說成：

　　　My elderly neighbors often give me candy.
　　　（年長的鄰居常給我糖果。）

　　　They usually give me little presents
　　　　or sweets.
　　　（他們常給我小禮物或糖果。）

　　　elderly〔'ɛldɚlɪ〕*adj.* 年長的
　　　candy〔'kændɪ〕*n.* 糖果
　　　present〔'prɛznt〕*n.* 禮物
　　　sweets〔swits〕*n. pl.* 糖果

7. **_There is a small park close by._**

small 〔 smɔl 〕 *adj.* 小的　　　park 〔 pɑrk 〕 *n.* 公園
close by 在附近

這句話的意思是「附近有座小公園。」close by
是地方副詞，作「在附近」(= *nearby*) 解，所以這句
話還可以說成：

There is a small park nearby. (附近有座小公園。)

There's a small park close to my home.
(我家附近有座小公園。)
【nearby 〔'nɪr'baɪ 〕 *adv.* 在附近　　**_close to_** 接近】

8. **_That's where I play with friends._**

這句話的意思是「那就是我和朋友一起玩的地方。」
這句話是從 That's **_the place_** where I play with
friends. 省略而來，where 在這裡是當關係副詞用，
而關係副詞是兼具連接詞作用的副詞，前面通常有名
詞當先行詞，但也可省略不寫，就像本句中省略了 the
place 一樣。

where 當關係副詞的用法，舉例如下：

Taipei is (the place) **_where_** I was born.
(台北是我出生的地方。)

National Taiwan University is **_where_** I want
to study. (國立台灣大學是我要唸的學校。)

be born 出生　　national 〔'næʃənl 〕 *adj.* 國立的
university 〔ˌjunə'vɝsətɪ 〕 *n.* 大學

○作文範例

My Neighborhood

My neighborhood is nice. I live in a high rise in the city. The location is convenient because everything we need is nearby. There are lots of shops and there is a small park right around the corner where I like to play. *Best of all*, I can walk to school in only a few minutes.

My neighbors are also nice. Everyone smiles and says hello. We all care about the community and keep it clean. I especially like my older neighbors. They are very sweet and they often give me treats. My neighborhood is special. It's my home and I never want to move.

6

● 中文翻譯

我 家 附 近

　　我家附近很不錯。我住在都市裡的一棟大廈。那個地點很方便，因為我們需要的一切都在附近。我家附近有很多商店，而且就在轉角附近，有座小公園，我很喜歡去那邊玩。最棒的是，我只要走幾分鐘就到學校了。

　　我的鄰居也都很親切。每個人都會微笑著打招呼。我們都很關心這個社區，並保持社區的整潔。我特別喜歡年長的鄰居。他們很親切，而且常常會給我甜點。我家附近很特別。這就是我的家，我從來都不會想搬家。

6

7. Protect the Environment

I'm worried about my country.
There is pollution everywhere.
It's time to do something about it.

We need fresh air to breathe.
We need pure water to drink.
We need a clean environment to be healthy.

People have to stop littering.
We have to respect our surroundings.
We must become friends of the earth.

7

protect〔prə'tɛkt〕 environment〔ɪn'vaɪrənmənt〕
worried〔'wɜɪd〕 country〔'kʌntrɪ〕
pollution〔pə'luʃən〕 everywhere〔'ɛvrɪˌhwɛr〕
need〔nid〕 fresh〔frɛʃ〕
air〔ɛr〕 breathe〔brið〕
pure〔pjʊr〕 clean〔klin〕
healthy〔'hɛlθɪ〕 litter〔'lɪtɚ〕
respect〔rɪ'spɛkt〕 surroundings〔sə'raʊndɪŋz〕
become〔bɪ'kʌm〕 earth〔ɝθ〕

***First*, *everyone must get involved*.**

Everyone must lend a hand.

Together we can clean up our
　neighborhoods.

Second, we can practice conservation.

We can reduce waste and reuse things.

We can recycle paper, bottles, and plastic.

Third, we can put up more "Don't litter"
　signs.

We can put trashcans on every corner.

We can pick up garbage when we see it.

involved (ɪn'vɑlvd)　　lend (lɛnd)
lend a hand　　　　together (tə'gɛðɚ)
neighborhood ('nebɚ,hʊd)
practice ('præktɪs)　　conservation (,kɑnsɚ've∫ən)
reduce (rɪ'djus)　　　waste (west)
reuse (ri'juz)　　　　recycle (ri'saɪkḷ)
bottle ('bɑtḷ)　　　　plastic ('plæstɪk)
sign (saɪn)　　　　　trashcan ('træ∫,kæn)
corner ('kɔrnɚ)　　　***pick up***
garbage ('gɑrbɪdʒ)

We must take action to fight pollution.
It's our future we're protecting.
It's our duty to keep our planet clean.

So, please don't pollute.
Don't be a litterbug.
Don't be afraid to remind others, too.

Let's protect nature's beauty.
Let's make our future bright.
Let's start to clean up now.

7

take (tek)

fight (faɪt)

protect (prə'tɛkt)

keep (kip)

pollute (pə'lut)

afraid (ə'fred)

nature ('netʃɚ)

bright (braɪt)

action ('ækʃən)

future ('fjutʃɚ)

duty ('djutɪ)

planet ('plænɪt)

litterbug ('lɪtɚ,bʌg)

remind (rɪ'maɪnd)

beauty ('bjutɪ)

start (stɑrt)

7. Protect the Environment

● 演講解說

I'm worried about my country.　　　　我很擔心我的國家。
There is pollution everywhere.　　　　到處都有污染。
It's time to do something about it.　　是該做點什麼的時候了。

We need fresh air to breathe.　　　　我們需要呼吸新鮮空氣。
We need pure water to drink.　　　　我們需要喝乾淨的水。
We need a clean environment to be　　我們需要整潔的環境，身
　healthy.　　　　　　　　　　　　　體才會健康。

7　People have to stop littering.　　　　人們必須停止亂丟垃圾。
We have to respect our　　　　　　　我們必須重視自己的周遭
　surroundings.　　　　　　　　　　環境。
We must become friends of the earth.　我們必須成為地球的朋友。

** ───────────

protect〔prəˋtɛkt〕v. 保護　environment〔ɪnˋvaɪrənmənt〕n. 環境
worried〔ˋwɝɪd〕adj. 擔心的　country〔ˋkʌntrɪ〕n. 國家
pollution〔pəˋluʃən〕n. 污染　fresh〔frɛʃ〕adj. 新鮮的
air〔ɛr〕n. 空氣　breathe〔brɪð〕v. 呼吸
pure〔pjʊr〕adj. 乾淨的　healthy〔ˋhɛlθɪ〕adj. 健康的
litter〔ˋlɪtɚ〕v. 亂丟垃圾　respect〔rɪˋspɛkt〕v. 尊重；重視
surroundings〔səˋraʊndɪŋz〕n. pl. 周遭環境
become〔bɪˋkʌm〕v. 變成　earth〔ɝθ〕n. 地球

First, *everyone must get involved*.	首先，每個人都必須參與。
Everyone must lend a hand.	每個人都必須幫忙。
Together we can clean up our neighborhoods.	我們可以一起把周圍打掃乾淨。
Second, we can practice conservation.	第二，我們要保護天然資源。
We can reduce waste and reuse things.	我可以減少浪費，並重複使用物品。
We can recycle paper, bottles, and plastic.	我們可以回收紙類、瓶子和塑膠。
Third, we can put up more "Don't litter" signs.	第三，我們可以多豎立一些「禁止亂丟垃圾」的告示。
We can put trashcans on every corner.	我們可以在每個轉角都放置垃圾桶。
We can pick up garbage when we see it.	我們可以在看到垃圾時，把它撿起來。

7

＊＊────────────

get〔gɛt〕v. 成爲（…的狀態）　　involved〔ɪnˋvɑlvd〕adj. 參與的
lend〔lɛnd〕v. 借出　　hand〔hænd〕n. 手；幫助　　*lend a hand* 幫助
clean up 打掃乾淨　　neighborhood〔ˋnebɚ͵hud〕n. 鄰近地區；周圍
reduce〔rɪˋdjus〕v. 減少　　waste〔west〕n. 垃圾；廢棄物
reuse〔riˋjuz〕v. 重複使用　　recycle〔riˋsaɪkḷ〕v. 回收
bottle〔ˋbɑtḷ〕n. 瓶子　　plastic〔ˋplæstɪk〕n. 塑膠
put up 張貼；豎立；建造　　sign〔saɪn〕n. 告示
trashcan〔ˋtræʃ͵kæn〕n. 垃圾桶　　corner〔ˋkɔrnɚ〕n. 角落
pick up 撿起　　garbage〔ˋgɑrbɪdʒ〕n. 垃圾

We must take action to fight pollution.
It's our future we're protecting.
It's our duty to keep our planet clean.

So, please don't pollute.
Don't be a litterbug.
Don't be afraid to remind others, too.

Let's protect nature's beauty.
Let's make our future bright.
Let's start to clean up now.

我們必須採取行動來對抗污染。
我們是在保護自己的未來。
我們有義務要保持地球的整潔。

所以，請不要製造污染。
不要亂丟垃圾。
也不要害怕提醒別人不要亂丟垃圾。

讓我們保護大自然的美。
讓我們把未來變得更有希望。
讓我們現在就開始打掃。

7

＊＊

take〔tek〕v. 採取　　action〔'ækʃən〕n. 行動
fight〔faɪt〕v. 對抗　　future〔'fjutʃɚ〕n. 未來
protect〔prə'tɛkt〕v. 保護
duty〔'djutɪ〕n. 義務　　keep〔kip〕v. 保持
planet〔'plænɪt〕n. 行星；地球　　pollute〔pə'lut〕v. 污染
litterbug〔'lɪtɚ͵bʌg〕n. 亂丟垃圾的人
afraid〔ə'fred〕adj. 害怕的　　remind〔rɪ'maɪnd〕v. 提醒
nature〔'netʃɚ〕n. 大自然　　beauty〔'bjutɪ〕n. 美
bright〔braɪt〕adj. 光明的；有希望的
start〔stɑrt〕v. 開始

● 背景說明

　　我們從小就被教導要做垃圾分類，在學校裡，還會看到不同顏色的垃圾桶，分別丟不同種類的垃圾。我們不能小看垃圾分類，它可是保護地球環境與資源的一大功臣。本篇演講稿就是要用英文教你作環保，讓你可以用英文談時事。

1. *There is pollution everywhere.*
pollution〔pəˈluʃən〕*n.* 污染
everywhere〔ˈɛvrɪˌhwɛr〕*adv.* 到處

　　這句話的意思是「到處都有污染。」
there is/are 不是「那裡」的意思，而是
「有」，例如：

7

> *There is* a book on the table.
> （桌上有一本書。）
>
> *There are* five people in my family.
> （我家有五個人。）
>
> *There are* forty students in my class.
> （我們班有四十個學生。）
>
> *There was* a fire near here last night.
> （昨晚這附近失火了。）

table〔ˈtebl̩〕*n.* 桌子　　class〔klæs〕*n.* 班級
fire〔faɪr〕*n.* 火災　　near〔nɪr〕*prep.* 在…附近

2. *It's time to do something about it.*

　　　　在本句中，第二個 it 指的是前一句提到的 pollution，所以這句話的意思是「是該做點什麼的時候了。」也可說成：

　　　Let's fix the problem now.
　　　（我們現在就來解決這個問題吧。）
　　　Let's take action now.
　　　（我們現在就採取行動吧。）

　　　fix〔fɪks〕v. 解決；處理
　　　problem〔'prabləm〕n. 問題
　　　take action 採取行動

　　　　另外，It is time to V. 的意思是「是該做…的時候了」，例如：

　　　It's time to have lunch.
　　　（吃午餐的時候到了。）
　　　It's time to do your homework.
　　　（是該做功課的時候了。）

　　　have〔hæv〕v. 吃　　lunch〔lʌntʃ〕n. 午餐
　　　homework〔'hom,wɝk〕n. 家庭作業；功課

3. *People have to stop littering.*
litter〔'lɪtɚ〕v. 亂丟垃圾

　　　　這句話的意思是「人們必須停止亂丟垃圾。」在本句中 litter 是當動詞，其用法跟我們在公共場所常看到的告示 No Littering.（禁止亂丟垃圾。）是一樣的。

另外，要特別注意 stop 的用法：

① stop + V-ing 作「停止（做某事）」解，例如：

Please **stop** wasting time; let's go.

（請停止浪費時間；我們走吧。）

② stop + to V. 作「停下來，然後去（做某事）」
解，例如：

Good drivers always **stop** to let people
　cross the road.

（優秀的駕駛人總是會把車停下來，讓人們過馬路。）

waste〔west〕v. 浪費　　driver〔'draɪvɚ〕n. 駕駛人
cross〔krɔs〕v. 橫越　　road〔rod〕n. 道路

4. *First, everyone must get involved.*

get〔gɛt〕v. 成爲（…的狀態）
involved〔ɪn'vɑlvd〕adj. 參與的

7

　　get 的基本意思是「拿到」，在此引申作「成爲
（…的狀態）」（= *become*）解，所以這句話的意思
是「首先，每個人都必須參與。」也可說成：

We all need to participate.

（我們都必須參與。）

Everyone has to take part.

（每個人都必須參與。）

need〔nid〕v. 必須
participate〔pɑr'tɪsə,pet〕v. 參與
take part 參加；參與

5. *Everyone must lend a hand.*
   lend〔lɛnd〕*v.* 借出　　hand〔hænd〕*n.* 幫助
   lend a hand 幫助（= *help*）

   　　　hand 的基本意思是「手」,在此引申作「幫助」
   （= *help*）解,lend a hand 的字面意思是「借出一隻
   手」,就像中文所說的「伸出援手」,在此引申爲「幫
   助」。所以這句話的意思是「每個人都必須幫忙。」也
   可說成：Each person must help.（每個人都必須
   幫忙。）

6. *Second, we can practice conservation.*
   practice〔'præktɪs〕*v.* 實行
   conservation〔ˌkɑnsəˈveʃən〕*n.*（天然資源的）保護

   　　　practice 的基本意思是「練習」,在此引申作
   「實行」解。這句話字面的意思是「第二,我們要
   實行保護天然資源。」也就是「第二,我們要保護
   天然資源。」也可說成：

   We have to protect the environment.
   （我們必須要保護環境。）
   We must make protecting the environment
   　　a habit.
   （我們必須要養成保護環境的習慣。）
   protect〔prəˈtɛkt〕*v.* 保護
   environment〔ɪnˈvaɪrənmənt〕*n.* 環境
   make〔mek〕*v.* 使成爲
   habit〔'hæbɪt〕*n.* 習慣

7. *Third, we can put up more "Don't litter" signs.*

　　put up 張貼；豎立；建造　　sign〔saɪn〕*n.* 告示

　　　　這句話的意思是「第三，我們可以多豎立一些『禁止亂丟垃圾』的告示。」也可說成：Third, we could place more "anti pollution" signs around. （第三，我們可以在附近多設一些「反污染」的告示牌。）

　　place〔ples〕*v.* 設置　　anti〔'æntɪ〕*adj.* 反對的

　　put up 在此是作「張貼；豎立；建造」解，例如：

> The fans ***put up*** a large sign to show their support.
> （歌迷豎起大型告示，來表達他們的支持。）

> They ***put up*** the Eiffel Tower in the middle of Paris.
> （他們在巴黎市中心建造了艾菲爾鐵塔。）

> fan〔fæn〕*n.* 迷　　large〔lardʒ〕*adj.* 大的
> show〔ʃo〕*v.* 表達　　support〔sə'port〕*n.* 支持
> Eiffel Tower〔'aɪfḷ'tauɚ〕*n.* 艾菲爾鐵塔
> middle〔'mɪdḷ〕*n.* 中間　　Paris〔'pærɪs〕*n.* 巴黎

8. *We can pick up garbage when we see it.*

　　pick up 撿起　　garbage〔'garbɪdʒ〕*n.* 垃圾

　　　　這句話的意思是「我們可以在看到垃圾時，把它撿起來。」也可說成：We should clean up trash whenever we see it. （每當我們看到垃圾時，都應該把它清乾淨。）【***clean up*** 清理乾淨　　trash〔træʃ〕*n.* 垃圾　　whenever〔hwɛn'ɛvɚ〕*conj.* 每當】

pick up 有幾個重要的意思，舉例如下：

① 作「撿起」解，例如：

He *picked up* his books.（他撿起他的書。）

② 作「搭載」解，例如：

Shall I *pick* you *up* at the station?

（要我去車站接你嗎？）

③ 作「購買」解，例如：

Mom *picked up* some fruit on her way home.

（媽媽在回家的路上買了一些水果。）

station〔'steʃən〕*n.* 車站

on one's *way home*　在某人回家的路上

7

9. *Don't be a litterbug.*

litterbug〔'lɪtɚ,bʌg〕*n.* 亂丟垃圾的人

　　這句話字面的意思是「不要當亂丟垃圾的人。」也就是「不要亂丟垃圾。」

　　bug〔bʌg〕是「小蟲」的意思，因爲污染環境的人，就跟蟲一樣，有害而且到處都是，所以美國人就叫亂丟垃圾的人 litterbug。

● 作文範例

Protect the Environment

There is a lot of pollution in my country. People litter and dirty the air and water. We need a clean environment in order to live healthy lives. We need fresh air to breathe and pure water to drink. *Therefore,* it is time to do something about this problem.

Everyone must get involved. *First,* we should clean up our neighborhoods. *Second,* we can recycle and reduce our garbage. *Third,* we can pick up trash whenever we see it. *Above all,* we must stop littering and keep our planet clean. In this way we can protect nature's beauty and give our children a good environment.

7

● 中文翻譯

保 護 環 境

　　我的國家有很多污染。人們亂丟垃圾，所以把空氣和水都弄髒了。為了要過著健康的生活，我們需要乾淨的環境。我們需要呼吸新鮮的空氣，還有飲用乾淨的水。因此，是該做點什麼來解決這個問題的時候了。

　　每個人都必須參與。首先，我們應該把周圍打掃乾淨。第二，我們可以做資源回收，減少垃圾。第三，當我們看到垃圾時，可以把它撿起來。最重要的是，我們必須停止亂丟垃圾，並且保持地球的乾淨。這樣，我們才能保護大自然的美，並給我們的孩子良好的環境。

7

8. My Strengths and Weaknesses

Self-awareness is important.
We need to know our good and bad points.
It's the best way to improve.

We should examine ourselves.
We should know who we are.
That's what true knowledge is.

Here are my strengths and weaknesses.
I want to share them with you.
Please listen and learn from me.

8

---

strength〔strɛŋθ〕　　　　weakness〔'wiknɪs〕
self-awareness〔ˌsɛlfə'wɛrnɪs〕
important〔ɪm'pɔrtn̩t〕　　　need〔nid〕
point〔pɔɪnt〕　　　　　　*good and bad points*
improve〔ɪm'pruv〕
examine〔ɪg'zæmɪn〕　　　true〔tru〕
knowledge〔'nɑlɪdʒ〕　　　share〔ʃɛr〕
listen〔'lɪsn̩〕　　　　　　learn〔lɜn〕

First, I'm healthy and fit.

I'm capable of working hard.

I seldom get sick.

My friends say I'm humble and polite.

I respect and obey my elders.

I like to help people whenever I can.

I'm also optimistic.

I have a confident personality.

I always look on the bright side of things.

8

healthy ('hɛlθɪ)   fit (fɪt)

capable ('kepəbḷ)   hard (hɑrd)

seldom ('sɛldəm)   get (gɛt)

sick (sɪk)   humble ('hʌmbḷ)

polite (pə'laɪt)   respect (rɪ'spɛkt)

obey (ə'be)   elder ('ɛldɚ)

whenever (hwɛn'ɛvɚ)   optimistic (ˌɑptə'mɪstɪk)

confident ('kɑnfədənt)   personality (ˌpɝsṇ'ælətɪ)

bright (braɪt)   side (saɪd)

look on the bright side of things

***On the other hand*, *I*'m *stubborn*.**

I'm a little impatient, too.

I sometimes whine and complain.

I watch too much TV.

I eat too much junk food.

And my room is often messy.

Nobody is perfect.

I'm not ashamed to admit it.

I just focus on improving myself.

---

on the other hand

impatient (ɪmˈpeʃənt)

whine (hwaɪn)

junk (dʒʌŋk)

messy (ˈmɛsɪ)

perfect (ˈpɝfɪkt)

admit (ədˈmɪt)

stubborn (ˈstʌbən)

sometimes (ˈsʌm͵taɪmz)

complain (kəmˈplen)

junk food

nobody (ˈno͵bɑdɪ)

ashamed (əˈʃemd)

focus (ˈfokəs)

8

8. My Strengths and Weaknesses

 演講解說

Self-awareness is important.	有自知之明很重要。
We need to know our good and bad points.	我們必須知道自己的優缺點。
It's the best way to improve.	那是使自己進步的最佳方式。
We should examine ourselves.	我們應該要檢討自己。
We should know who we are.	我們應該要了解自己。
That's what true knowledge is.	那才是真正的知識。
Here are my strengths and weaknesses.	以下就是我的優缺點。
I want to share them with you.	我要把我的優缺點告訴你們。
Please listen and learn from me.	請聽我說，並從我的身上學習。

8

** ———————————

strength〔strɛŋθ〕*n.* 優點　　weakness〔'wiknɪs〕*n.* 缺點
self-awareness〔͵sɛlfə'wɛrnɪs〕*n.* 自知；自覺
important〔ɪm'pɔrtn̩t〕*adj.* 重要的　　need〔nid〕*v.* 必須；需要
point〔pɔɪnt〕*n.* 點　　*good and bad points* 優缺點
improve〔ɪm'pruv〕*v.* 改善；進步
examine〔ɪg'zæmɪn〕*v.* 檢查；檢討　　true〔tru〕*adj.* 真正的
knowledge〔'nɑlɪdʒ〕*n.* 知識　　share〔ʃɛr〕*v.* 分享；告訴
listen〔'lɪsn̩〕*v.* 聽　　learn〔lɜn〕*v.* 學習

First, *I'm healthy and fit.*　　　首先，我很健康。

I'm capable of working hard.　　我可以很努力工作。

I seldom get sick.　　　　　　　我很少生病。

My friends say I'm humble　　　　我的朋友說我謙虛有禮。
　and polite.

I respect and obey my elders.　　我尊重長輩，而且會聽他們的話。

I like to help people whenever　　我隨時都喜歡幫助別人。
　I can.

I'm also optimistic.　　　　　　我也很樂觀。

I have a confident personality.　我的個性充滿自信。

I always look on the bright　　　我總是看事物的光明面。
　side of things.

**

healthy〔'hɛlθɪ〕*adj.* 健康的　　fit〔fɪt〕*adj.* 健康的

capable〔'kepəbḷ〕*adj.* 能夠…的　　seldom〔'sɛldəm〕*adv.* 很少

get〔gɛt〕*v.* 變成　　sick〔sɪk〕*adj.* 生病的

get sick 生病　　humble〔'hʌmbḷ〕*adj.* 謙虛的

polite〔pə'laɪt〕*adj.* 有禮貌的　　respect〔rɪ'spɛkt〕*v.* 尊重

obey〔ə'be〕*v.* 服從；順從　　elder〔'ɛldə〕*n.* 長輩

whenever〔hwɛn'ɛvə〕*conj.* 無論何時；每當

also〔'ɔlso〕*adv.* 也　　optimistic〔ˌɑptə'mɪstɪk〕*adj.* 樂觀的

confident〔'kɑnfədənt〕*adj.* 有自信的

personality〔ˌpɜsṇ'ælətɪ〕*n.* 個性

bright〔braɪt〕*adj.* 光明的　　side〔saɪd〕*n.* 面

look on the bright side of things 看事物的光明面

8

On the other hand, **I'm stubborn**.	另一方面，我很固執。
I'm a little impatient, too.	我也有點沒耐心。
I sometimes whine and complain.	我有時候會發牢騷和抱怨。
I watch too much TV.	我看太多電視。
I eat too much junk food.	我吃太多垃圾食物。
And my room is often messy.	還有我的房間常常很亂。
Nobody is perfect.	沒有人是完美的。
I'm not ashamed to admit it.	我不會不好意思承認這件事。
I just focus on improving myself.	我只關心如何使自己進步。

8

** ─────────────

on the other hand 在另一方面　　stubborn〔ˈstʌbɚn〕*adj.* 固執的
impatient〔ɪmˈpeʃənt〕*adj.* 沒耐心的
sometimes〔ˈsʌmˌtaɪmz〕*adv.* 有時候　　whine〔hwaɪn〕*v.* 發牢騷
complain〔kəmˈplen〕*v.* 抱怨　　junk〔dʒʌŋk〕*n.* 垃圾
junk food 垃圾食物　　messy〔ˈmɛsɪ〕*adj.* 雜亂的
nobody〔ˈnoˌbɑdɪ〕*pron.* 沒有人　　perfect〔ˈpɝfɪkt〕*adj.* 完美的
ashamed〔əˈʃemd〕*adj.* 不好意思的；感到羞恥的
admit〔ədˈmɪt〕*v.* 承認
focus〔ˈfokəs〕*v.* 集中（注意力、關心）< *on* >
improve〔ɪmˈpruv〕*v.* 改善；使進步

◐ 背景說明

　　每個人都有自己的優缺點，即使是品學兼優的好學生，也會有缺點，像是個性可能比較固執，所以人緣不太好。每個人都有進步的空間，只要你懂得檢討自己，你就會變得更完美。

1. ***Self-awareness is important.***
   self-awareness〔͵sɛlfəˈwɛrnɪs〕*n.* 自知；自覺
   important〔ɪmˈpɔrtn̩t〕*adj.* 重要的

   　　這句話的意思是「有自知之明很重要。」aware 的意思是「知道的」，所以 self-awareness 就是「自知」或「了解自己」的意思。

   這句話也可說成：

   　　It's useful and beneficial to know yourself.
   　　（了解自己是大有助益的。）

   　　To know your strengths and weaknesses
   　　　is essential.
   　　（知道自己的優缺點很重要。）

   　　useful〔ˈjusfəl〕*adj.* 有益的；有用的
   　　beneficial〔͵bɛnəˈfɪʃəl〕*adj.* 有益的
   　　strength〔strɛnθ〕*n.* 優點
   　　weakness〔ˈwiknɪs〕*n.* 缺點
   　　essential〔əˈsɛnʃəl〕*adj.* 必要的；非常重要的

8

2. *We should know who we are.*

這句話的字面意思是「我們應該知道自己是誰。」
引申為「我們應該要了解自己。」也可說成：

We should understand ourselves.
（我們應該要了解自己。）

We should be aware of ourselves.
（我們應該要認識自己。）

understand〔͵ʌndɚˋstænd〕 *v.* 了解
aware〔əˋwɛr〕 *adj.* 知道的　　***be aware of*** 知道；認識到

3. *First, I'm healthy and fit.*

healthy〔ˋhɛlθɪ〕 *adj.* 健康的　　　fit〔fɪt〕 *adj.* 健康的

　　fit 的基本意思是「適合的」，也可作「身材穠纖
合度的」或「健康的」解。healthy 大多指身體內部
的健康，而 fit 則用來指身材或外表的健康，本句同
時用 healthy 和 fit，除了指內外都健康，還有強調
非常健康的意思，所以這句話要翻成「首先，我很
健康。」也可說成：

I'm in excellent physical condition.
（我的身體狀況很好。）

I'm fit as a fiddle.（我很健康。）

excellent〔ˋɛksḷənt〕 *adj.* 極好的
physical〔ˋfɪzɪkḷ〕 *adj.* 身體的
condition〔kənˋdɪʃən〕 *n.* 狀況　　fiddle〔ˋfɪdḷ〕 *n.* 小提琴
(***as***) ***fit as a fiddle*** 非常健康的

8

4. *I seldom get sick.*

seldom〔ˈsɛldəm〕*adv.* 很少　　get〔gɛt〕*v.* 變得
sick〔sɪk〕*adj.* 生病的　　***get sick*** 生病

這句話的意思是「我很少生病。」seldom 是作
「很少」(= *rarely*) 解，所以這句話也可以說成：

I rarely fall ill.（我很少生病。）

I hardly ever catch a cold or fall sick.
（我很少感冒或生病。）

rarely〔ˈrɛrlɪ〕*adv.* 很少
fall〔fɔl〕*v.* 變成（…的狀態）　　ill〔ɪl〕*adj.* 生病的
fall ill 生病（ = *fall sick* = *get sick* ）
hardly〔ˈhɑrdlɪ〕*adv.* 幾乎不；很少
hardly ever 幾乎不；很少　　***catch a cold*** 感冒

下面都是美國人常說的話：

He *seldom* eats fish.（他很少吃魚。）

My parents *seldom* lose their temper.
（我爸媽很少發脾氣。）

She *seldom* showed her feelings.
（她很少表達自己的感受。）

fish〔fɪʃ〕*n.* 魚　　parents〔ˈpɛrənts〕*n. pl.* 父母
lose〔luz〕*v.* 失去　　temper〔ˈtɛmpɚ〕*n.* 脾氣
lose one's ***temper*** 發脾氣　　show〔ʃo〕*v.* 表現
feeling〔ˈfilɪŋ〕*n.* 感受

8

5. ***I have a confident personality.***

confident〔ˈkɑnfədənt〕*adj.* 有自信的
personality〔ˌpɝsṇˈælətɪ〕*n.* 個性

　　這句話的意思是「我的個性充滿自信。」也可
說成：

I'm a self-assured person.
（我是個有自信的人。）

I'm sure of myself.
（我對自己很有自信。）

self-assured〔ˌsɛlfəˈʃur〕*adj.* 有自信的
sure〔ʃur〕*adj.* 確定的；有自信的

　　當你要自我介紹時，可以多用一些好的形容詞
來說明自己的個性，例如：

① sweet〔swit〕*adj.* 甜美的；溫柔的

② polite〔pəˈlaɪt〕*adj.* 有禮貌的

③ bright〔braɪt〕*adj.* 開朗的

④ optimistic〔ˌɑptəˈmɪstɪk〕*adj.* 樂觀的

⑤ sensitive〔ˈsɛnsətɪv〕*adj.* 敏感的

⑥ friendly〔ˈfrɛndlɪ〕*adj.* 友善的

⑦ carefree〔ˈkɛrˌfri〕*adj.* 無憂無慮的

⑧ liberal〔ˈlɪbərəl〕*adj.* 開明的

⑨ cheerful〔ˈtʃɪrfəl〕*adj.* 開朗的

⑩ happy-go-lucky〔ˈhæpɪˌgoˈlʌkɪ〕*adj.* 樂天的

6. *I always look on the bright side of things.*

bright〔braɪt〕*adj.* 光明的　　side〔saɪd〕*n.* 面
look on the bright side of things 看事物的光明面

　　　　這句話的意思是「我總是看事物的光明面。」也
可說成：

　　　I'm an extremely optimistic person.
　　　（我是個非常樂觀的人。）
　　　I'm an idealist.
　　　（我是個理想主義者。）

　　　extremely〔ɪk'strimlɪ〕*adv.* 非常
　　　optimistic〔͵ɑptə'mɪstɪk〕*adj.* 樂觀的
　　　person〔'pɝsn̩〕*n.* 人
　　　idealist〔aɪ'dɪəlɪst〕*n.* 理想主義者

　　　look on the bright side of things 的意思是
「看事物的光明面；對事物抱持著樂觀的態度」，
例如：

　　　When depressed, try to *look on the bright
　　　　side of things.*
　　　（當你沮喪的時候，要試著看看事物的光明面。）
　　　It's very healthy to *look on the bright side
　　　　of things.*
　　　（對事物抱持著樂觀的態度是很健康的。）

　　　depressed〔dɪ'prɛst〕*adj.* 沮喪的
　　　healthy〔'hɛlθɪ〕*adj.* 健康的

8

7. **I'm not ashamed to admit it.**

ashamed〔ə'ʃemd〕*adj.* 不好意思的；感到羞恥的
admit〔əd'mɪt〕*v.* 承認

　　　這句話的意思是「我不會不好意思承認這件事。」
ashamed 是作「不好意思的；感到羞恥的」解，例如：

He was **ashamed** to ask a favor.
（他不好意思請人幫忙。）

He is **ashamed** of his failure.
（他以自己的失敗爲恥。）

favor〔'fevɚ〕*n.* 幫忙　　failure〔'feljɚ〕*n.* 失敗

8. **I just focus on improving myself.**

focus〔'fokəs〕*v.* 集中（注意力、關心）< *on* >
improve〔ɪm'pruv〕*v.* 改善；使進步

　　　這句話的意思是「我只關心如何使自己進步。」
focus 的基本意思是「焦點」，在此當動詞用，作
「集中（注意力、關心）」（= *concentrate*）解，
這句話也可說成：

I just concentrate on becoming better.
（我只專注於讓自己變得更好。）

I just pay attention to correcting my faults.
（我只注意改正自己的缺點。）

concentrate〔'kɑnsn̩ˏtret〕*v.* 專心；專注
attention〔ə'tɛnʃən〕*n.* 注意（力）
pay attention to 注意
correct〔kə'rɛkt〕*v.* 改正　　fault〔fɔlt〕*n.* 缺點

8

○ 作文範例

My Strengths and Weaknesses

It is important to know our good and bad points because this knowledge will help us to improve. We should examine ourselves and learn who we are. *Above all*, we should recognize our strengths and weaknesses. *For example*, I am healthy and fit, so I can work hard. I'm also optimistic, humble and polite. These are my strengths. *However*, I also have weaknesses. *For one thing*, I'm stubborn and a little impatient. I'm sometimes lazy as well and can spend a whole day just watching TV and eating junk food. I'm not ashamed to admit these bad points. Knowing what they are lets me focus on improving myself.

8

● 中文翻譯

我的優缺點

　　知道自己的優缺點是很重要的，因為知道這件事，有助於使我們進步。我們應該要檢討自己，並且知道自己是什麼樣的人。最重要的是，我們應該要認清自己的優缺點。例如，我很健康，所以可以很努力工作。還有我很樂觀、謙虛和有禮貌。這些是我的優點。但是，我也有缺點。首先，我很固執，而且有點沒耐心。我有時候也很懶惰，會花一整天的時間，只是看看電視和吃垃圾食物。我不會不好意思承認這些缺點。知道這些缺點，會讓我注意如何使自己進步。

9. My Views on Inner Beauty

I want to talk about beauty.
I have a favorite story.
It's The Ugly Duckling.

There was an unattractive duck.
It was born looking different.
It suffered a childhood of teasing.

However, as it grew, the duck changed.
Its inner beauty emerged.
It turned into a lovely swan.

view〔vju〕
beauty〔'bjutɪ〕
ugly〔'ʌglɪ〕
unattractive〔͵ʌnə'træktɪv〕
different〔'dɪfərənt〕
childhood〔'tʃaɪld͵hʊd〕
however〔haʊ'ɛvɚ〕
change〔tʃendʒ〕
lovely〔'lʌvlɪ〕

inner〔'ɪnɚ〕
favorite〔'fevərɪt〕
duckling〔'dʌklɪŋ〕
duck〔dʌk〕
suffer〔'sʌfɚ〕
teasing〔'tizɪŋ〕
grow〔gro〕
emerge〔ɪ'mɝdʒ〕
swan〔swɑn〕

9

I love the message of this story.
It's that we gain beauty as we grow.
We only have to believe in ourselves.

Our appearance is important.
A natural healthy look is wonderful.
But inner beauty is more than good looks.

True beauty comes from the heart.
It comes from our personality,
   attitude and spirit.
It's how we feel, act and treat others.

message〔'mɛsɪdʒ〕	gain〔gen〕
grow〔gro〕	believe〔bə'liv〕
appearance〔ə'pɪrəns〕	important〔ɪm'pɔrtn̩t〕
natural〔'nætʃərəl〕	healthy〔'hɛlθɪ〕
look〔lʊk〕	wonderful〔'wʌndɚfəl〕
more than	true〔tru〕
come from	heart〔hɑrt〕
personality〔ˌpɝsn̩'ælətɪ〕	attitude〔'ætəˌtjud〕
spirit〔'spɪrɪt〕	act〔ækt〕
treat〔trit〕	

9

Everyone has some beauty.

Everyone has special charm.

We're all attractive in different ways.

So don't misjudge what beauty is.

Don't be fooled by what you see.

All that glitters is not gold.

Remember we're all like that duck.

We're slowly becoming swans.

We just have to let that beauty shine.

special ('spɛʃəl)	charm (tʃɑrm)
attractive (ə'træktɪv)	different ('dɪfərənt)
way (we)	misjudge (mɪs'dʒʌdʒ)
fool (ful)	glitter ('glɪtɚ)
gold (gold)	***All that glitters is not gold***.
remember (rɪ'mɛmbɚ)	like (laɪk)
slowly ('sloli)	become (bɪ'kʌm)
let (lɛt)	shine (ʃaɪn)

9

9. My Views on Inner Beauty

演講解說

I want to talk about beauty.	我想要談談美。
I have a favorite story.	我很喜歡一個故事。
It's The Ugly Duckling.	就是醜小鴨的故事。
There was an unattractive duck.	有隻鴨子長得不好看。
It was born looking different.	牠天生就看起來不太一樣。
It suffered a childhood of teasing.	牠童年時受到許多嘲笑。
However, as it grew, the duck changed.	但是，當這隻鴨子長大時，牠開始有了改變。
Its inner beauty emerged.	牠的內在美顯現出來。
It turned into a lovely swan.	牠變成了一隻美麗的天鵝。

9

** ————————————————————

view〔vju〕*n.* 看法
inner〔'ɪnɚ〕*adj.* 內在的　　beauty〔'bjutɪ〕*n.* 美
unattractive〔͵ʌnə'træktɪv〕*adj.* 不漂亮的　　duck〔dʌk〕*n.* 鴨
different〔'dɪfərənt〕*adj.* 不同的　　suffer〔'sʌfɚ〕*v.* 遭受
childhood〔'tʃaɪld͵hʊd〕*n.* 童年時期
teasing〔'tizɪŋ〕*n.* 嘲笑　　however〔haʊ'ɛvɚ〕*adv.* 然而
change〔tʃendʒ〕*v.* 改變　　emerge〔ɪ'mɝdʒ〕*v.* 顯現
lovely〔'lʌvlɪ〕*adj.* 可愛的；美麗的　　swan〔swɑn〕*n.* 天鵝

I love the message of this story.	我很喜歡這個故事的寓意。
It's that we gain beauty as we grow.	那就是我們會愈長大愈漂亮。
We only have to believe in ourselves.	只是我們必須要相信自己。
Our appearance is important.	我們的外表很重要。
A natural healthy look is wonderful.	擁有自然而健康的外表很棒。
But inner beauty is more than good looks.	但是內在美比容貌好看還重要。
True beauty comes from the heart.	眞正的美是發自內心。
It comes from our personality, attitude and spirit.	它是來自於我們的個性、態度和心靈。
It's how we feel, act and treat others.	它是我們的感受、行爲,還有對待別人的方式。

** ———————————

message〔'mɛsɪdʒ〕*n.* 寓意;主旨
gain〔gen〕*v.* 得到;增加　　believe〔bə'liv〕*v.* 相信
believe in 相信…是好的　　appearance〔ə'pɪrəns〕*n.* 外表
important〔ɪm'pɔrtn̩t〕*adj.* 重要的
natural〔'nætʃərəl〕*adj.* 自然的　　healthy〔'hɛlθɪ〕*adj.* 健康的
look〔lʊk〕*n.* 外表　　wonderful〔'wʌndəfəl〕*adj.* 極好的;很棒的
more than 不只是…而已　　looks〔lʊks〕*n. pl.* 容貌
true〔tru〕*adj.* 眞正的　　***come from*** 來自
heart〔hɑrt〕*n.* 心　　personality〔ˌpɜsn̩'ælətɪ〕*n.* 個性
attitude〔'ætəˌtjud〕*n.* 態度　　spirit〔'spɪrɪt〕*n.* 心;精神
act〔ækt〕*v.* 行爲;舉止　　treat〔trit〕*v.* 對待

9

***Everyone has some beauty*.**　　　每個人都有某種美。
Everyone has special charm.　　　每個人都有特殊的魅力。
We're all attractive in different　　我們都有不同的吸引力。
　　ways.

So don't misjudge what beauty is.　所以不要誤解美麗的意思。
Don't be fooled by what you see.　不要被你所看到的東西給騙了。
All that glitters is not gold.　　　閃閃發光者，未必都是黃金；
　　　　　　　　　　　　　　　　不可以貌取人。

Remember we're all like that duck.　記住，我們都像那隻鴨子。
We're slowly becoming swans.　　我們會慢慢變成天鵝。
We just have to let that beauty　　我們只須讓美麗顯露出來。
　　shine.

＊＊ ────────────────

special〔'spɛʃəl〕*adj.* 特別的　　charm〔tʃɑrm〕*n.* 魅力
attractive〔ə'træktɪv〕*adj.* 有吸引力的
different〔'dɪfərənt〕*adj.* 不同的　　way〔we〕*n.* 方面
misjudge〔mɪs'dʒʌdʒ〕*v.* 判斷錯誤　　fool〔ful〕*v.* 欺騙；愚弄
glitter〔'glɪtɚ〕*v.* 閃閃發光　　gold〔gold〕*n.* 黃金
***All that glitters is not gold*.**　【諺】閃閃發光者，未必都是黃金；
　　不可以貌取人。
remember〔rɪ'mɛmbɚ〕*v.* 記住　　like〔laɪk〕*prep.* 像
slowly〔'slolɪ〕*adv.* 緩慢地　　become〔bɪ'kʌm〕*v.* 變成
let〔lɛt〕*v.* 讓　　shine〔ʃaɪn〕*v.* 顯露；發光

9

◉背景說明

　　內在美指的是光看外表，看不到的優點和特質，像是心地善良，或是脾氣溫和等等。雖然外表很重要，但是內在的光華，才是幫助你成功的真正關鍵。本篇演講稿，要用醜小鴨的故事，來告訴你內在美的真正含意。

1. **It's The Ugly Duckling.**
ugly〔'ʌglɪ〕*adj.* 醜的
duckling〔'dʌklɪŋ〕*n.* 小鴨

　　這句話的意思是「就是醜小鴨的故事。」醜小鴨的作者是安徒生，他是十九世紀最偉大的童話大師，他一生寫了一百六十四則童話，包括拇指姑娘、小美人魚、國王的新衣和賣火柴的小女孩，都是他的作品。

2. **It was born looking different.**
be born 出生　　look〔luk〕*v.* 看起來
different〔'dɪfərənt〕*adj.* 不同的

　　這句話的意思是「他天生就看起來不太一樣。」在本句中 looking different 是當主詞補語，補充說明 It，所以這句話還可說成：It looked strange at birth. (他出生時就看起來很奇怪。)
strange〔strendʒ〕*adj.* 奇怪的
birth〔bɜθ〕*n.* 出生　　**at birth** 出生時

9

現在分詞（V-ing）當補語用的例子還有：

They went along *singing* merrily.

（他們一邊走一邊開心地唱歌。）

The boy came *running* to meet me.

（那個男孩跑來迎接我。）

go along 前進　　merrily〔ˋmɛrɪlɪ〕*adv.* 愉快地
meet〔mit〕*v.* 迎接

【比較】 分詞是具有形容詞作用的動詞型態，其中現在分詞
　　　　雖然長得跟動名詞一樣，但用法卻不同，例如：

She sat up *reading* last night.

（她昨晚熬夜讀書。）

【reading 是現在分詞，修飾 She，為主詞補語】

I enjoy *reading* comic books.（我喜歡看漫畫書。）

【reading 是動名詞，做 enjoy 的受詞】

sit up 熬夜　　*last night* 昨晚
enjoy〔ɪnˋdʒɔɪ〕*v.* 喜歡　　comic〔ˋkɑmɪk〕*adj.* 漫畫的

3. *Its inner beauty emerged.*

inner〔ˋɪnɚ〕*adj.* 內在的　　beauty〔ˋbjutɪ〕*n.* 美
emerge〔ɪˋmɝdʒ〕*v.* 顯現

這句話的意思是「牠的內在美顯現出來。」emerge
是作「顯現」（= *appear*）解，所以這句話也可說成：
Its inner loveliness came out.（牠的內在美顯現
出來。）

appear〔əˋpɪr〕*v.* 出現；顯現
loveliness〔ˋlʌvlɪnɪs〕*n.* 美麗；可愛
come out 顯現；出現

4. *It turned into a lovely swan.*

   turn into 變成   lovely〔'lʌvlɪ〕*adj.* 可愛的；美麗的
   swan〔swɑn〕*n.* 天鵝

這句話的意思是「牠變成了一隻美麗的天鵝。」也可說成：It became a beautiful swan.（牠變成了一隻美麗的天鵝。）

turn into 是作「變成」(= *become*) 解，例如：

   The water ***turned into*** ice.
   （水變成冰了；水結成冰。）

   The shy new student soon ***turned into*** a
      talkative boy.
   （那名害羞的新生很快就變成了愛講話的男孩。）

   Our trip ***turned into*** a nightmare after all
      our money was stolen.
   （在所有的錢被偷走之後，我們的旅行就變成了
      一場惡夢。）

   ice〔aɪs〕*n.* 冰   shy〔ʃaɪ〕*adj.* 害羞的
   soon〔sun〕*adv.* 很快地
   talkative〔'tɔkətɪv〕*adj.* 喜歡說話的
   trip〔trɪp〕*n.* 旅行
   nightmare〔'naɪt,mɛr〕*n.* 惡夢
   steal〔stil〕*v.* 偷【三態變化爲：steal-stole-stolen】

9

5. *I love the message of this story.*

message〔'mεsɪdʒ〕 *n.* 寓意；主旨

　　message 的基本意思是「訊息」，在此作「寓意；主旨」(= *moral*) 解，所以這句話的意思是「我很喜歡這個故事的寓意。」也可說成：

I really enjoy the moral of this story.
（我眞的很喜歡這個故事的寓意。）

I really like the main point of this story.
（我眞的很喜歡這個故事的主旨。）

moral〔'mɔrəl〕 *n.* 寓意
main〔men〕 *adj.* 主要的
point〔pɔɪnt〕 *n.* 要點

message 在以下的句子裡，都是作「寓意；主旨」解：

What *message* do you think the novel has?
（你認爲那部小說的寓意是什麼？）

The movie has a serious *message*.
（這部電影的主題很嚴肅。）

I get the *message*.（我明白了。）

novel〔'nɑvḷ〕 *n.* 小說
movie〔'muvɪ〕 *n.* 電影
serious〔'sɪrɪəs〕 *adj.* 嚴肅的
get〔gεt〕 *v.* 了解；明白

6. *But inner beauty is more than good looks.*

looks〔lʊks〕*n. pl.* 容貌

　　look 的基本意思是「看」，在此當名詞用，looks
作「容貌」解，所以這句話的字面意思是「但是內在
美不只是容貌好看而已。」引申為「但是內在美比容
貌好看還重要。」

7. *Don't be fooled by what you see.*

fool〔ful〕*v.* 欺騙；愚弄

　　fool 的基本意思是「愚笨的」，在此當動詞用，
作「欺騙；愚弄」解，所以這句話的意思是「不要
被你所看到的東西給騙了。」

下面都是美國人常說的話，我們按照使用頻率排列：

Don't judge a book by its cover.【第一常用】
(【諺】勿以貌取人。)

Appearances can be deceiving.【第二常用】
(【諺】外表會騙人。)

Don't let your eyes trick you.【第三常用】
(不要讓你的眼睛把你給矇騙了。)

Don't be fooled by appearances.【第四常用】
(不要被外表給騙了。)

judge〔dʒʌdʒ〕*v.* 判斷　　cover〔'kʌvɚ〕*n.* 封面
appearance〔ə'pɪrəns〕*n.* 外表
deceiving〔dɪ'sivɪŋ〕*adj.* 欺騙的　　trick〔trɪk〕*v.* 欺騙

9

8. *All that glitters is not gold.*

glitter〔'glɪtɚ〕*v.* 閃閃發光　　gold〔gold〕*n.* 黃金

All that glitters is not gold. 【諺】閃閃發光者，未必都是黃金；不可以貌取人。

這句話是十八世紀時，英國詩人湯瑪士‧格雷（Thomas Gray）說的，字面意思是「閃閃發光者，未必都是黃金。」就是告誡大家，不可以貌取人的意思，也可說成：Beautiful things aren't always good.（美麗的東西未必是好的。）【*not always*　未必；不一定】

9. *We just have to let that beauty shine.*

let〔lɛt〕*v.* 讓　　shine〔ʃaɪn〕*v.* 顯露；發光

shine 的基本意思是「發光」，但在此作「顯露」解，所以這句話的意思是「我們只須讓美麗顯露出來。」也可說成：We must allow our inner beauty to radiate.（我們必須讓內在美散發出來。）

【allow〔ə'laʊ〕*v.* 讓　　radiate〔'redɪ,et〕*v.* 散發出來】

另外，let 是使役動詞，所以接受詞後，只能接原形動詞，例如：

Please *let* me try one more time.
（請讓我再試一次。）

Let me tell you the interesting story.
（讓我告訴你那個有趣的故事。）

try〔traɪ〕*v.* 嘗試　　time〔taɪm〕*n.* 次
interesting〔'ɪntrɪstɪŋ〕*adj.* 有趣的

● 作文範例

My Views on Inner Beauty

People today are very concerned about appearances. *However*, in my opinion, inner beauty is more than good looks. A natural, healthy look is nice, but true beauty comes from the heart. It depends on our personality, attitude and spirit. It can be seen in how we treat others.

Everyone has beauty, but we are all attractive in different ways. It is important to understand what true beauty is so that we are not fooled by what we see. All that glitters is not gold, and sometimes we have to look beyond appearances in order to see beauty. We must also let our own inner beauty shine through.

9

● 中文翻譯

我對內在美的看法

現在的人都很關心外表。但是，依我之見，內在美比容貌好看還重要。擁有自然而健康的外表很好，但是真正的美是發自內心的。真正的美是取決於我們的個性、態度和心靈。真正的美可以從我們對待別人的方式看出來。

每個人都是美麗的，但是我們都有不同的吸引力。了解真正的美是什麼很重要，因為這樣我們才不會被所看到的東西給騙了。閃閃發光者，未必都是黃金，而且有時候我們必須看外表以外的東西，才能看到真正的美。我們也要讓自己的內在美顯露出來。

9

10. Win or Lose, Be a Good Sport

I'd like to talk about sportsmanship.
Here is a quote I want to start with.
It's "Win or lose, be a good sport."

That means always play fair.
Always follow the rules.
Always be honest and polite.

We have competitions every day.
We face challenges every moment.
We compete with others all the time.

win〔wɪn〕   lose〔luz〕
win or lose   sport〔sport〕
sportsmanship〔'sportsmən,ʃɪp〕
quote〔kwot〕   mean〔min〕
fair〔fɛr〕   follow〔'falo〕
rule〔rul〕   honest〔'anɪst〕
polite〔pə'laɪt〕   competition〔,kampə'tɪʃən〕
face〔fes〕   challenge〔'tʃælɪndʒ〕
moment〔'momənt〕 compete〔kəm'pit〕

10

When we win, **we should be humble**.
We should put ourselves in the others'
 shoes.
We should understand how they feel.

We can compliment our opponents.
We can give them an encouraging word.
We can say, "You did a great job, too."

Remain silent and modest.
Never gloat or be too proud.
Enjoy the victory, but don't rub it in.

humble〔'hʌmbḷ〕   shoes〔ʃuz〕
understand〔͵ʌndɚ'stænd〕   feel〔fil〕
compliment〔'kɑmplə͵mɛnt〕
opponent〔ə'ponənt〕
encouraging〔ɪn'kɝɪdʒɪŋ〕
remain〔rɪ'men〕   silent〔'saɪlənt〕
modest〔'mɑdɪst〕   gloat〔glot〕
proud〔praʊd〕   victory〔'vɪktrɪ〕
rub〔rʌb〕

10

When we lose, ***we should be gracious***.

We should put our disappointment aside.

We should congratulate the winner sincerely.

No one likes to lose.

But it's a chance to learn more.

We should be thankful for the experience.

Life is like a game.

Sometimes we win; sometimes we lose.

A good attitude will make us winners

    for life.

gracious ('greʃəs)

disappointment (ˌdɪsə'pɔɪntmənt)

aside (ə'saɪd)   ***put ~ aside***

congratulate (kən'grætʃəˌlet)

winner ('wɪnɚ)   sincerely (sɪn'sɪrlɪ)

like (laɪk)   chance (tʃæns)

thankful ('θæŋkfəl)   experience (ɪk'spɪrɪəns)

game (gem)   sometimes ('sʌmˌtaɪmz)

attitude ('ætəˌtjud)   make (mek)

for life

10

10. Win or Lose, Be a Good Sport

○ 演講解說

I'd like to talk about sportsmanship.	我想要談談運動家精神。
Here is a quote I want to start with.	我想要引用以下這句話作為開場白。
It's "Win or lose, be a good sport."	就是「不論輸贏，都要當個出色的運動家。」
That means always play fair.	意思是一定要光明正大地比賽。
Always follow the rules.	一定要遵守規則。
Always be honest and polite.	一定要誠實而且有禮貌。
We have competitions every day.	我們每天都會面臨競爭。
We face challenges every moment.	我們時時刻刻都會面臨挑戰。
We compete with others all the time.	我們經常要和別人競爭。

**　** ———

win〔wɪn〕*v.* 贏　　lose〔luz〕*v.* 輸　　***win or lose*** 不論輸贏
sport〔sport〕*n.* 輸得起的人；運動家
sportsmanship〔'sportsmən,ʃɪp〕*n.* 運動家精神
quote〔kwot〕*n.* 引用句　　play〔ple〕*v.* 比賽
fair〔fɛr〕*adv.* 公正地；光明正大地　　follow〔'falo〕*v.* 遵守
rule〔rul〕*n.* 規則　　honest〔'anɪst〕*adj.* 誠實的
polite〔pə'laɪt〕*adj.* 有禮貌的
competition〔,kampə'tɪʃən〕*n.* 競爭　　face〔fes〕*v.* 面對；面臨
challenge〔'tʃælɪndʒ〕*n.* 挑戰　　compete〔kəm'pit〕*v.* 競爭

10

When we win, ***we should be humble***.	贏的時候，我們應該要謙虛。
We should put ourselves in the others' shoes.	我們應該站在別人的立場想。
We should understand how they feel.	我們應該了解他們的感受。
We can compliment our opponents.	我們可以讚美對手。
We can give them an encouraging word.	我們可以對他們說句鼓勵的話。
We can say, "You did a great job, too."	我們可以說：「你表現得也很好。」
Remain silent and modest.	要保持沉默與謙虛。
Never gloat or be too proud.	絕對不要幸災樂禍，或是驕傲。
Enjoy the victory, but don't rub it in.	要享受勝利，但不要一直提到別人的失敗。

＊＊ ────────────

humble〔ˈhʌmbḷ〕*adj.* 謙虛的　shoes〔ʃuz〕*n. pl.* 鞋子

put *oneself* ***in*** *a person's* ***shoes*** 站在別人的立場想

compliment〔ˈkɑmpləˌmɛnt〕*v.* 稱讚

opponent〔əˈponənt〕*n.* 對手　give〔gɪv〕*v.* 給；對～說

encouraging〔ɪnˈkɝɪdʒɪŋ〕*adj.* 鼓勵的

word〔wɝd〕*n.* 話；詞句　remain〔rɪˈmen〕*v.* 保持

silent〔ˈsaɪlənt〕*adj.* 沉默的　modest〔ˈmɑdɪst〕*adj.* 謙虛的

gloat〔glot〕*v.* 幸災樂禍　proud〔praʊd〕*adj.* 驕傲的

victory〔ˈvɪktrɪ〕*n.* 勝利　rub〔rʌb〕*v.* 摩擦

rub it in 不停提到別人的失敗；反覆地講

10

When we lose, we should be gracious.
We should put our disappointment
aside.
We should congratulate the winner
sincerely.

No one likes to lose.
But it's a chance to learn more.

We should be thankful for the
experience.

Life is like a game.
Sometimes we win; sometimes
we lose.
A good attitude will make us
winners for life.

輸的時候，我們應該要優雅。
我們應該要拋開失望。

我們應該要誠心誠意地恭喜
優勝者。

沒有人喜歡輸。
但那是個讓你學到更多東西
的機會。
我們應該要感謝這個經驗。

人生就像一場比賽。
我們有時候會贏；有時候
會輸。
良好的心態會使我們成爲終
生的贏家。

** —————————————

gracious〔'greʃəs〕*adj.* 優雅的
disappointment〔,dɪsə'pɔɪntmənt〕*n.* 失望
aside〔ə'saɪd〕*adv.* 在一邊地
put～aside 把～丟到一邊；把～拋諸腦後
congratulate〔kən'grætʃə,let〕*v.* 恭喜　　winner〔'wɪnɚ〕*n.* 優勝者
sincerely〔sɪn'sɪrlɪ〕*adv.* 眞誠地　　like〔laɪk〕*v.* 喜歡　*prep.* 像
chance〔tʃæns〕*n.* 機會　　thankful〔'θæŋkfəl〕*adj.* 感謝的
experience〔ɪk'spɪrɪəns〕*n.* 經驗　　attitude〔'ætə,tjud〕*n.* 心態
make〔mek〕*v.* 使成爲　***for life*** 終生

10

背景說明

　　本篇演講稿主要是在討論運動家精神。所謂運動家精神，就是要光明正大地參加比賽，然後在比賽時，拿出勇氣，堅持到最後一秒，並在得知結果之後，秉持著「勝不驕，敗不餒」的精神，誠心讚美與恭賀對手。

1. *I'd like to talk about sportsmanship.*
   talk about 談論
   sportsmanship〔'sportsmən,ʃɪp〕*n.* 運動家精神

   　　這句話的意思是「我想要談談運動家精神。」也可說成：I want to talk about being a good sport.（我想要談談如何當個出色的運動家。）
   【sport〔sport〕*n.* 輸得起的人；運動家】

   　　would like 是作「想要」解，跟 want（想要）的差別是，用 would like 的語氣比較溫和有禮，例如：

   I ***would like*** to buy a new cell phone.
   （我想要買一支新手機。）

   My dad ***would like*** to lose a few pounds.
   （我爸想要減個幾磅。）

   I'***d like*** to go to the movies with my boyfriend.
   （我想要跟男朋友去看電影。）

   cell phone 手機　　lose〔luz〕*v.* 減少（體重）
   pound〔paund〕*n.* 磅　　***go to the movies*** 去看電影
   boyfriend〔'bɔɪ,frɛnd〕*n.* 男朋友

10

2. ***Win or lose, be a good sport.***

win〔wɪn〕*v.* 贏　　　lose〔luz〕*v.* 輸
win or lose　不論輸贏
sport〔sport〕*n.* 輸得起的人；運動家

　　　sport 的基本意思是「運動」，在此引申爲「輸得起的人；運動家」，而當 a good sport 作「輸得起的人」解時，其相反詞爲 a poor sport（輸不起的人）。

　　　這句話可以翻成「不論輸贏，都要當個輸得起的人。」或「不論輸贏，都要當個出色的運動家。」還可説成：

In sports, no matter what, be polite!
（參加比賽的時候，無論如何，都要有禮貌！）

Be a humble winner; be a gracious loser;
　always play fair.
（要當個謙虛的贏家；要當個優雅的輸家；
　　一定要光明正大地比賽。）

sport〔sport〕*n.* 運動；競賽
no matter what　無論如何
polite〔pə'laɪt〕*adj.* 有禮貌的
humble〔'hʌmbḷ〕*adj.* 謙虛的
winner〔'wɪnɚ〕*n.* 贏家
gracious〔'greʃəs〕*adj.* 優雅的
loser〔'luzɚ〕*n.* 輸家　　play〔ple〕*v.* 比賽
fair〔fɛr〕*adv.* 公平地；光明正大地

3. *We face challenges every moment.*

face〔fes〕*v.* 面對　　challenge〔'tʃælɪndʒ〕*n.* 挑戰

moment〔'momənt〕*n.* 時刻

every moment 時時刻刻

這句話的意思是「我們時時刻刻都會面臨挑戰。」every moment 是作「時時刻刻」(= *all the time*) 解。這句話也可以説成：

Everyone encounters daily tests.

（每個人每天都會碰到考驗。）

We all have to deal with constant
　challenges.

（我們都必須要應付不斷的挑戰。）

encounter〔ɪn'kaʊntɚ〕*v.* 遭遇；碰見

daily〔'delɪ〕*adj.* 日常的；每天的

test〔tɛst〕*n.* 考驗　　*deal with* 應付

constant〔'kɑnstənt〕*adj.* 不斷的

另外，face 的基本意思是「臉」，是當名詞用，但在這裡是當動詞用，作「面對」(= *confront*) 解，例如：

I can't *face* myself. （我無法面對自己。）

Always *face* your problems — never
　avoid them.

（一定要面對你的問題 — 絕不可逃避問題。）

problem〔'prɑbləm〕*n.* 問題

avoid〔ə'vɔɪd〕*v.* 逃避

10

4. *We compete with others all the time.*
compete〔kəm'pit〕*v.* 競爭　　*all the time* 經常；總是

　　這句話的意思是「我們經常要和別人競爭。」
all the time 是作「經常；總是」(＝*constantly*)
解，例如：

　　Our class leader studies *all the time.*
　　（我們班的班長總是在唸書。）

　　I feel like my parents nag me *all the time.*
　　（我覺得我的父母好像經常對我嘮叨。）

　　Nobody likes him because he cries and
　　　complains *all the time.*
　　（沒有人喜歡他，因為他經常哭鬧和抱怨。）

leader〔'lidə〕*n.* 領袖　　*feel like* 覺得像
parents〔'pɛrənts〕*n. pl.* 父母　　nag〔næg〕*v.* 對～嘮叨
nobody〔'no‚badɪ〕*pron.* 沒有人　　like〔laɪk〕*v.* 喜歡
cry〔kraɪ〕*v.* 哭　　complain〔kəm'plen〕*v.* 抱怨

5. *We should put ourselves in the others' shoes.*
shoes〔ʃuz〕*n. pl.* 鞋子
put oneself in a person's shoes 站在別人的立場想

10

　　這句話的意思是「我們應該站在別人的立場想。」
put *oneself* in *a person's* shoes 是源自美洲土著印
地安人的說法，他們認爲你要先穿那個人的鞋走一段
路之後，才有資格評斷那個人，後來就引申爲「站在
別人的立場想」或「替別人設身處地著想」的意思。

6. *We can give them an encouraging word.*

give〔gɪv〕*v.* 給；對～說
encouraging〔ɪn'kɝɪdʒɪŋ〕*adj.* 鼓勵的
word〔wɝd〕*n.* 話；詞句

　　這句話的意思是「我們可以對他們說句鼓勵的話。」
give 的主要意思是「給」，在此引申為「對～說」
(= *tell*)，而 word 的基本意思是「字」，在此指「話；
詞句」。這句話也可說成：We can say something
nice to them. (我們可以對他們說些好話。)

如果你贏了比賽，記得對對手說些鼓勵的話，例如：

You're an excellent player. (你是個優秀的選手。)
You're a tough opponent. (你是個強勁的對手。)
You deserved to win, too. (你也應該要贏的。)

excellent〔'ɛkslənt〕*adj.* 優秀的　　player〔'pleɚ〕*n.* 選手
tough〔tʌf〕*adj.* 強硬的；難應付的
opponent〔ə'ponənt〕*n.* 對手
deserve〔dɪ'zɝv〕*v.* 值得；應得

如果你輸了，也要有風度地恭賀贏家，例如：

Congratulations on your win. (恭喜你獲勝。)
Your team is really good. (你的隊伍非常出色。)
I wish I could play as well as you.
(我希望我可以打得跟你一樣好。)

congratulations〔kən,grætʃə'leʃənz〕*n. pl.* 恭喜
win〔wɪn〕*n.* 勝利；贏　　team〔tim〕*n.* 隊伍
wish〔wɪʃ〕*v.* 希望　　play〔ple〕*v.* 參加 (比賽)
as…as～　和～一樣…

10

7. ***We can say*, *"You did a great job, too."***

great〔gret〕*adj.* 很棒的　　job〔dʒɑb〕*n.* 工作；事情

　　　這句話的意思是「我們可以說:『你表現得也很好。』」
do a good job 的說法,在字典上都查不到,字典上只有
make a good job (幹得好),但是美國人很少這樣說。
所以下次你要誇讚別人表現得很好時,記得要說 You
did a great job. (你表現得很好。)

8. ***Enjoy the victory*, *but don't rub it in*.**

victory〔'vɪktrɪ〕*n.* 勝利　　rub〔rʌb〕*v.* 摩擦
rub it in 不停提到別人的失敗；反覆地講

　　　這句話的意思是「要享受勝利,但不要一直提到別人
的失敗。」rub 本身是「摩擦」的意思,而 rub it in 從字
面上看,就像我們跌倒瘀青時,要邊擦藥邊揉一揉,明明
會痛還是要揉,後來這個片語就引申為「不停提到別人的
失敗」,意思就是攻擊別人的痛處,這句話還可說成:

Never remind people of their failures or
　　mistakes. (不要提醒別人他們的失敗或錯誤。)

It's OK to celebrate success but never tease
　　the losers. (慶祝成功很好,但是絕不能嘲笑輸家。)

remind〔rɪ'maɪnd〕*v.* 提醒
remind sb. of sth. 提醒某人某事
mistake〔mə'stek〕*n.* 錯誤
celebrate〔'sɛlə,bret〕*v.* 慶祝
success〔sək'sɛs〕*n.* 成功
tease〔tiz〕*v.* 嘲笑　　loser〔'luzɚ〕*n.* 失敗者；輸家

10

Win or Lose, Be a Good Sport

Sportsmanship is important. Whether we win or lose, we must be good sports. That means we must follow the rules of the game and always play fair. This is true not only in sports, but also in life. We face competitions and challenges every day. When we succeed, we should be modest. We can enjoy the victory, but we must not rub it in. *Instead*, we should compliment our opponents or give them an encouraging word. *On the other hand*, when we lose, we should be gracious. We should forget our disappointment and congratulate the winner. No one likes to lose, but we should be thankful for the experience. A good attitude will make us winners for life.

10

● 中文翻譯

不論輸贏，都要當個出色的運動家

運動家的精神很重要。不管我們是輸或贏，都必須要當個出色的運動家。意思就是我們必須要遵守比賽的規則，而且一定要光明正大地比賽。不只是在比賽時要這樣，在人生中也是。我們每天都要面臨競爭和挑戰。當我們成功時，應該要謙虛。我們可以享受勝利，但不要一直提到別人的失敗。相反地，我們應該要讚美對手，或是對他們說句鼓勵的話。另一方面，當我們輸的時候，也應該要優雅。我們應該要忘記自己的失望，並恭喜優勝者。沒有人喜歡輸，但是我們應該要感謝這樣的經驗。良好的心態會使我們成為終生的贏家。

這10篇演講稿，
你都背下來了嗎？
現在請利用下面的提示，
不斷地複習。

以下你可以看到每篇演講稿的格式，三句為一組，九句為一段，每篇演講稿共三段，27句，看起來是不是輕鬆好背呢？不要猶豫，趕快開始背了！每篇演講稿只要能背到50秒之內，就終生不忘！

1. My Favorite Class

My favorite class is gym.
I can't wait for PE.
It's really fun, fun, fun.

I love to get out of class.
I need a break from books.
It feels great to move around.

We all look forward to it.
It's a chance to unwind.
It's like an escape to freedom.

We have gym twice a week.
We wear T-shirts and shorts.
We play both inside and out.

PE starts off with exercise.
We stretch, bend and twist.
It's always important to warm up.

We do jumping jacks.
We do push-ups and sit-ups.
Then we jog around the track.

Finally, the real fun begins.
We divide into teams.
We play sports and compete.

I like basketball and dodge ball.
I enjoy badminton and ....
Soccer is the most exciting to me.

Win or lose, it's OK.
There's no pressure at all.
That's why I love gym class ....

2. My Favorite Holiday

My favorite holiday is New Year.
Westerners call it Chinese ....
We call it Lunar New Year.

It's a big celebration.
It's an important festival.
It's the highlight of the year.

New Year comes during winter.
It's cold and chilly then.
But our hearts are warm and ....

We follow old customs.
We stick red couplets beside our ....
We clean up and sweep out our ....

Everyone returns home.
Families get together.
We chat and have a big feast.

People visit each other.
We greet relatives and neighbors.
We exchange best wishes and gifts.

It's a super time for kids.
We get presents and treats.
We set off fireworks, too.

Best of all are red envelopes.
They're gifts of money.
We all love them the most.

New Year is a time to give thanks.
We're grateful and happy.
We expect a great year ahead.

3. My Summer Vacation

Hurray for July!
Three cheers for August!
I love the summertime.

No school for two months.
No worrying about tests.
And a lot less homework to do.

I get to do what I want.
I'm as free as a bird.
It's my dream come true.

Summer is a chance to relax.
I read interesting books.
I watch my favorite TV programs.

I hang out with my friends.
We roam around the neighborhood.
We enjoy staying up late.

I visit my grandparents.
I travel with my family.
We take fun trips all around.

Summer is a time to learn more.
I try to improve my weak areas.
I try to learn something new.

Last summer, I took swimming ….
This summer, I might join a ….
Maybe I'll study computers or ….

Remember summer days fly by fast.
The vacation is over too soon.
So do as much as you can.

4. My Grandparents

My grandparents are so sweet.
They hold a special place in my ….
They're more precious than gold.

They worked hard all their lives.
They sacrificed for my family.
They raised my parents very well.

I owe them thanks and praise.
I'm alive because of them.
I don't know how to repay them.

My grandparents are special ….
They're easygoing and ….
They're easier to talk to than my ….

My grandma makes me delicious ….
My grandpa takes me fishing ….
They are wonderful babysitters ….

They are full of wisdom, too.
They explain right and wrong.
They teach me to be honest and fair.

Gram and gramps are family ….
They carry on old traditions.
They pass on stories of our ….

My grandparents hold my ….
They keep everyone in harmony.
Every family member cherishes ….

I never take them for granted.
I know they won't live forever.
But they'll always be a part of ….

5. My Favorite Pet

My favorite pets are dogs.
I smile when I see one.
I play with them when I can.

Dogs aren't animals to me.
They're perfect companions.
They're man's best friends.

Dogs are loyal and honest.
Their eyes are like windows.
I can see right into their hearts.

Dogs are unique.
No two are alike.
Each one has its own personality.

The little ones are cute.
The big ones are frisky.
Their wagging tails are funny.

I love shaggy dogs.
I love playful dogs.
I wouldn't mind being a dog.

Dogs are bright.
They can do tricks.
They can be useful, too.

Guide dogs lead the blind.
Rescue dogs save people.
Search dogs help the police.

Dogs know how to live.
They're happy-go-lucky.
I hope I can have one someday.

6. My Neighborhood

My neighborhood is nice.
It's my home sweet home.
I feel comfortable there.

I live in the city.
My home is in a high rise.
It's quiet, safe and clean.

The location is convenient.
Everything we need is nearby.
I can walk to school in minutes.

My neighbors are friendly.
Everyone is kind and polite.
Everyone smiles and says hello.

We watch out for each other.
We care about the environment.
We always hold cleanup activities.

I like the older neighbors best.
They are gentle and sweet.
They often give me food and ….

There is a small park close by.
It has a new playground.
That's where I play with friends.

My community is special.
It's perfect to me.
I'd never want to move.

How's your neighborhood?
Do you like where you live?
I hope you love your home, too.

7. Protect the Environment

I'm worried about my country.
There is pollution everywhere.
It's time to do something about it.

We need fresh air to breathe.
We need pure water to drink.
We need a clean environment to ....

People have to stop littering.
We have to respect our ....
We must become friends of the ....

First, everyone must get involved.
Everyone must lend a hand.
Together we can clean up our ....

Second, we can practice ....
We can reduce waste and reuse ....
We can recycle paper, bottles ....

Third, we can put up more ....
We can put trashcans on every ....
We can pick up garbage when ....

We must take action to fight ....
It's our future we're protecting.
It's our duty to keep our planet ....

So, please don't pollute.
Don't be a litterbug.
Don't be afraid to remind others ....

Let's protect nature's beauty.
Let's make our future bright.
Let's start to clean up now.

8. My Strengths and Weaknesses

Self-awareness is important.
We need to know our good and ....
It's the best way to improve.

We should examine ourselves.
We should know who we are.
That's what true knowledge is.

Here are my strengths and ....
I want to share them with you.
Please listen and learn from me.

First, I'm healthy and fit.
I'm capable of working hard.
I seldom get sick.

My friends say I'm humble ....
I respect and obey my elders.
I like to help people ....

I'm also optimistic.
I have a confident personality.
I always look on the bright ....

On the other hand, I'm stubborn.
I'm a little impatient, too.
I sometimes whine and complain.

I watch too much TV.
I eat too much junk food.
And my room is often messy.

Nobody is perfect.
I'm not ashamed to admit it.
I just focus on improving myself.

9. *My Views on Inner Beauty*

I want to talk about beauty.
I have a favorite story.
It's The Ugly Duckling.

There was an unattractive duck.
It was born looking different.
It suffered a childhood of teasing.

However, as it grew, the duck ….
Its inner beauty emerged.
It turned into a lovely swan.

I love the message of this story.
It's that we gain beauty as we grow.
We only have to believe in ….

Our appearance is important.
A natural healthy look is wonderful.
But inner beauty is more than ….

True beauty comes from the heart.
It comes from our personality ….
It's how we feel, act and treat ….

Everyone has some beauty.
Everyone has special charm.
We're all attractive in different ….

So don't misjudge what beauty is.
Don't be fooled by what you see.
All that glitters is not gold.

Remember we're all like that duck.
We're slowly becoming swans.
We just have to let that beauty shine.

10. *Win or Lose, Be a Good Sport*

I'd like to talk about ….
Here is a quote I want to start with.
It's "Win or lose, be a good sport."

That means always play fair.
Always follow the rules.
Always be honest and polite.

We have competitions every day.
We face challenges every moment.
We compete with others all the time.

When we win, we should be ….
We should put ourselves in the ….
We should understand how they ….

We can compliment our opponents.
We can give them an ….
We can say, "You did a great job ….

Remain silent and modest.
Never gloat or be too proud.
Enjoy the victory, but don't rub it in.

When we lose, we should be ….
We should put our ….
We should congratulate the ….

No one likes to lose.
But it's a chance to learn more.
We should be thankful for the ….

Life is like a game.
Sometimes we win; sometimes we ….
A good attitude will make us ….

本書所有人

「一口氣兒童英語演講②」背誦記錄表

篇　　　　　　　名	口試通過日期	口試老師簽名
1. My Favorite Class	年　　月　　日	
2. My Favorite Holiday	年　　月　　日	
3. My Summer Vacation	年　　月　　日	
4. My Grandparents	年　　月　　日	
5. My Favorite Pet	年　　月　　日	
6. My Neighborhood	年　　月　　日	
7. Protect the Environment	年　　月　　日	
8. My Strengths and Weaknesses	年　　月　　日	
9. My Views on Inner Beauty	年　　月　　日	
10. Win or Lose, Be a Good Sport	年　　月　　日	
全部10篇演講總複試	年　　月　　日	

　　自己背演講，很難專心，背給別人聽，是最有效的方法。練習的程序是：自己背➡背給同學聽➡背給老師聽➡在全班面前發表演講。可在教室裡、任何表演舞台或台階上，二、三個同學一組練習，比賽看誰背得好，效果甚佳。

　　天天聽著CD，模仿美國人的發音和語調，英文自然就越說越溜。英語演講背多後，隨時都可以滔滔不絕，口若懸河。